DREAM JOB

WACKY ADVENTURES OF AN HR MANAGER

Janet Garber

ISBN: 978-1-4834-4747-6 (sc)
ISBN: 978-1-4834-4746-9 (e)

Last rev. date: 3/11/2016

But these were mere crises and what are crises, compared to all that never stops, knows neither ebb nor flow, its surface leaden above internal depths. (Samuel Beckett, *Molloy*)

To my two lovable guys,
Sheldon I. Hanner and Elie A. Fouéré

CONTENTS

CHAPTER I

METRO, BOULOT, DODO
(TRAIN, JOB, BEDDY-BYE)

To the question, "How's it going?" the French sigh and respond: Metro (Train), Boulot (Job), Dodo (Beddy Bye), which is simply their way of saying, "Same old, same old . . ."

There he was! Ponytail Man/PTM. Melie spotted him through the window as she was running across the New Rochelle platform to the Metro North train.

The good thing about being a klutz, or at least a bit off balance, was that she didn't have to fake falling into his lap.

"Sorry. Sorry!" she said as she scrambled into the seat opposite his.

She had never been this close to him before—the lacquered nails, the pointy Italian leather shoes, the beautifully tailored suit that fit his tall, lean muscular frame like a second skin. And of course the dirty blond hair, luxuriant, swept into a thick ponytail. He looked to be in his late forties—he had a faint scent of the sixties, the strange and the hippie. Her type.

She'd been watching him for over a year. Now was her chance.

"What do you think of the book?" Melie, queen of pickup lines, asked. She smiled sweetly and tried not to let her chin tremble too much when she spoke.

"Oh, this? Piece of crap!"

Succinct. A man of few words. The strong, silent type.

1

"I kinda liked it," she ventured.

"Deviant. Dangerous. Dreadful."

Alliterative critique. He must be bright. She stared at his forehead, longing to reach out to smooth the stray blond hairs from his perfect brow. She watched as he pushed the hair back himself, catching the telltale glint on his finger. *Oh no!*

Wedding rings on the train always struck her as a personal affront. They hurt her eyes—solid gold bands, so boring really, thrust into her line of vision, folding the *Times*, whipping out the commuter ticket at the conductor's voice, popping out of leather gloves like maladroit rabbits just when you least expected it, like a slap of cold water in the face.

"You're not wanted here," they seemed to scream out at her, a sound like spoons striking the sides of a stack of wineglasses:

> We don't want you.
> We don't need you.
> You're not wanted here.
> DING.

The Ponytail Man seemed to register the change in the weather. He took a long look—she fidgeted. He leaned in so she did too.

"You know, you're not a bad-looking chick. What did you say your name was?"

"Melanie . . . Melie."

"Seriously, Mel, the book is well crafted. It held my interest. But those sex scenes, huh? Not too likely. Not many girls will do those things—without being paid." He chuckled to himself. Then, leaning in even closer (she could smell his cologne), he whispered, "Would you?"

Hmm. Yep. You bet. Can't wait. Have been waiting so long. Too long. Forever. I could cry . . .

She backed up, grabbed her coat, scarf, hat, gloves.

"My stop! Bye now."

Exiting, she knew she'd just have to wait for the next train. She was one stop short. If he'd ever even noticed her before, he'd know she got off at Grand Central Station, the same as everybody.

She walked to a bench and sat on the edge, miles away from a bleary-eyed drunk.

"You're so pretty."

"Oh, shoot me now," she muttered to herself as she glared down the tracks, willing the next train to appear.

It was one of those winter days in December when a piss-yellow light slanted in through the scabrous pock-marked train windows, marking the passengers' faces with disease, plague, early death . . .

. . . one of those days when buses, cars, trucks, motorcycles, bicycles, on her walk to work, emerged from their usual collective dead roar to reach a crescendo of individualized screeching, snarling, and caterwauling. Even passing nannies pushing squeaky-wheeled strollers made sounds that grated straight through the side of her head into her brain.

. . . a day when someone opening the outer door and squeezing past before she could enter, was too close, much too dangerously close for too many seconds.

. . . a day when her coffee was not dark at all, really quite light, with a suspicious taste of sugar that impelled her to rehearse scenes of (no doubt) unjustifiable homicide, coupled with mutilation of one neighborhood coffee vendor.

Some days were like this, she knew. But still she longed to crawl deeper inside her skin, to retract somehow, to close her eyes so she could pretend she wasn't really there. Or the world wasn't.

(She always did this at the GYN's. If she couldn't see her nakedness and him, conjoined in the same room, neither could he. Or so it seemed. She sometimes did that in bed too with a new man. She then got to do something that really wasn't happening, so it was all right.)

She was out of sorts this day, not well in her skin, as the French say. A bad fit, they meant, like a snake shedding its skin overnight being a little too tight in its new one the next morning.

But she did not have the type of job (woe is she) where she could just slink back under a rock or vanish behind a cloud or disappear in a poof. For Melie was the employment/employee relations manager at the world-class Axis Mundi Medical Center. Such a prestigious job. A dream job, really. But she was paid to be visible. She was the Point Man. That was the whole point.

After a short subway ride and a longish walk, she pushed open the door to Axis Mundi Medical Center's Employment Office. First one in, she hung up her coat, made a bathroom stop, clutched her leaky cup and took it to her office to sip. Patches of white paper from the boss lady and pink scraps from everyone else littered her desk to protest loudly her absence of the week before. Where had she been? How had she survived? What were they supposed to do without her?

I went cross-country skiing for the first time. For my 40th birthday. So there!

Sukie, her senior recruitment coordinator, who was a full decade past retirement age, lumbered in to tell her the major plots brewing, all variations on one theme really, and which fires she and Geena, the junior recruitment coordinator, had managed to stomp out themselves. Of course they had done it all wrong, and stoked and fanned where they should have dropped and rolled. Melie could almost smell the smoldering embers in the bush.

Sukie needed to be the savior of every situation. She was all about maximizing the drama. Having been a single mother of six, she was used to hopping from crisis to crisis. Though a college dropout, she could talk the talk and marched into meetings with the doctors, passing herself off as an alumnae of a well-respected New York City university. Gracious, maternal, a little larger than life, a little bit of a fruitcake, she managed to flutter and prance and preen in such a way that many at the Axis Mundi turned to her for advice; some, because Sukie was in her seventies, mistook her for Melie's boss. That was fine with Melie.

Geena was brand spanking new, an Amazon queen, tall, blonde, beautiful, sheltered, from the suburbs. She was still under Sukie's spell though somewhat shocked by some of Sukie's less orthodox maneuvers, like making applicants wait an hour in Reception before she'd interview them.

Arielle, the third member of Melie's staff, the receptionist, was just out of college, sweet, clueless and more than a little taken aback by all the fireworks in the Employment Office. How long would she last?

And Melie, what was she? Still single, a good-enough-looking girl of slight build, unruly dark hair, buttoned up to save her life, fearful that her

One Big Secret would undo her and that she could not forever contain the combustion building within . . .

Staff meeting over, Melie bid her staff adieu. "Do your worst!" They trundled out. She stared down at her blank grey desk blotter calendar. No one was allowed to book appointments for her, lest said appointments interfere with her ability to respond to any and all crises. She rested her eyes in the blankness.

For Melie was no less than chief of the Mop-Up Crew (a/k/a human resources). She was the designated problem solver at Axis Mundi Medical Center, tasked with cleaning up any and all messes made by employees, administrators, technicians, principal investigators, doctors, visitors, vendors, street urchins, and so on.

She did not want to see too many doctors in person today. She hoped she could do a fast job on their administrators, preferably over the phone, and leave them holding the bag—for a change. She picked up the first message and quickly let it drop.

Dr. Kohan, gastro chief, stood in the doorway to her office. *Ambushed after all.* She gestured for him to have a seat. "Melie, Melie, you've got to help me," Dr. Kohan whined before his bottom even hit the chair. His round cherubic face was all crinkly and worried.

"That's what I'm here for," Melie quipped gaily. "What seems to be the problem today?"

She had become over time her own best caricature. Who were her role models? Dr. Joyce Brothers? Imus' crazy psychiatrist character? Various movie shrinks? She had only taken two psych courses in her life. Thank God one of them was abnormal.

"You know, I've had this secretary, Lois, working with me for the past year. . . . Oh, how I wish I had Rosie back again!"

"Dr. Kohan, do you think it's fair to compare? Rosie was with you for eighteen years."

"Oh, I know that. Oy, do I know! Tell me what to do. What am I going to do?"

Melie looked at the notes she'd been scribbling, then said, "Bernie, you haven't really told me yet what the problem is with Lois. Is she late, excessively absent, possibly insubordinate? Does she give good messages?"

Dr. Kohan perked up for a minute, then shook his head sadly.

After a few more go-rounds, Melie was no closer to understanding. She nevertheless advised the following: "Stop doing her typing for her. That's her job. Your job is to patch up people's *kishkas*. Can you do that for me? Then, if we see she can't type, we'll be able to get the goods on her and fire her."

Dr. Kohan seemed untouched by her ministrations but tiredly agreed and, thankfully, left her office.

Only later did she find out—from Sukie—the real problem: that Rosie had given a lot more than good messages those eighteen years, especially when a patient cancelled the last appointment of the day.

Melie barely had time for a bathroom break when she was confronted with another walk-in, a secretary from cardiothoracic, looking so distraught, Melie quickly ushered her into her office.

"She pinches me, Melie. She comes up and pinches me on the arm. I can't take it anymore!"

"That's not . . . right."

"Once, you know, she came up behind me and started choking me. I had to go to employee health. I had bruises."

"What was that?" Melie got up off her chair and walked around her desk to get a better picture of Barbara Freedman, taking in her middle-aged tired eyes, disappearing waistline, the pixie-cut faded blonde hair, framing a once-pretty face.

"She's always calling me names, telling me no one will hire me because I'm too fat and ugly and old. I'm not so ugly, am I?"

"Wh . . . why didn't you make a complaint earlier, Babs, when this first happened?

"I was scared of losing my job. I need this job. I have to support my mother and myself. What's going to happen?"

Melie returned to her seat, amazed that after ten years she was still running into situations she'd never encountered before. "Let me see what I can do." She scribbled on a pad.

"I'm afraid of her, Melie. Last week she told me she bought a gun. Why did she tell me that?"

"Take it easy, Babs. Let me make some inquiries about Dr. Needles."

"Don't use my name!"

"I'll try not to use your name."

"Get me out of there, will you? Get me a transfer."

Uh-oh. Academics behaving badly, Melie observed, as she ushered Babs out of her office. A whole different set of rules, not the ones she was used to, governed the inevitable investigation. Melie would have to involve the Dean of HR, her boss, Terry K. Quincent, whose face had all the appeal of standing dishwater before you rinse the dishes in it. Neither hot nor cold enough to be interesting. On some days a few suds snuck in and then Melie almost dared hope. She continued to look every day for those errant suds. But they vanished so quickly she decided she'd been fooling herself. Lank silver hair clung to both sides of the square do-business face. More than anything Melie minded the absence of color. It was provocative somehow. Insulting.

The body itself was basically squat though with womanly curves she sabotaged by walking like a boxer or garage mechanic from the Midwest. All Melie needed was for her to crawl out from under her car, wipe her smudgy face on her sleeve and declare, "It's the alternator." She'd put on display her bitten dirt-rimmed nails when handing Melie the invoice. . .

In real life her nails were cut bluntly across the top. She wore dresses that hung from the shoulder or shirtwaist outfits emphasizing her bulky rear end, formidable hips and shelf-like stomach. The worst was her voice: like a mortar shell on bad days, and on others, like a rabid Cujo barking.

When she entered a room and ran towards Melie, Melie instinctively backed away. She couldn't help it. Her boss looked like she could run any-thing over. She looked like she proceeded on tracks. She was a Sherman tank. She was a bulldog. She was "Merry Terry."

Melie had already been steeling herself for an I'm-Next-to-Jump-Out-the-Window day when word reached her that Merry Terry was on the rampage. Before picking up the receiver, she uttered a little prayer: "Please-please-please don't make this another problem!"

To no avail. Arielle was whispering over the intercom, "Mel, she's coming—she can't find a file. Or something. Oops . . ." The phone went dead.

Seconds later Merry Terry barreled in, wildly waving a form in her hand, and marched around the desk to tower her four-foot-nine-inch frame over Melie. Actually, she was four-foot-ten on all sides.

"Can you explain how (stamping her foot)—why (slamming fist down on desk)—on what continent (spitting now) this is considered proper procedure?"

Melie noticed Merry Terry's neck had gone all splotchy red—normally not a positive sign. Sukie had followed Merry Terry in and rolled her eyes at Melie when she noticed the rash. She ran up to them, tottering on her wobbly high heels.

"Oh, I can explain the last one, Dean Terry. John Folkes, a good friend of mine, asked if we could waive the background check for this lovely young woman he met last weekend at Dr. Tamis' party in the Hamptons. She comes from a fine family, you know, and—"

"And what were you going to put down on Form 155b, pray tell?" Merry Terry snapped.

"Oh, you see, I . . ." Here Sukie looked over at Melie for the answer.

"Sukie!" Melie said, shaking her head.

"Sorry, I'll run it now. Is that all?"

"Not quite. That's not why I'm here. What have you done with Geraldo Gutierrez?"

Geena waltzed in, humming. Noticing the scene, she nevertheless asked gaily, "Oh, did I do anything wrong?"

"Get lost!" said Merry Terry. Then she turned to Sukie. "You too!"

Sukie mumbled an excuse and tottered away with Geena right behind her.

Merry Terry pounded her small round fist on Melie's desk. "Melie, I told you when you were hired ten years ago that you needed to fire Sukie. You haven't done it."

"Terry, it's just that . . . she has her good points. And the only thing you had on her was her lateness—after so many years!"

With a dismissive harrumph, Merry Terry turned on her haunches and directed her one-woman stampede down the hall toward the Benefits Office. "Get your group to find Geraldo's file!" She yelled over her shoulder. Then in a stage whisper, "God, I hate Employment."

The Employment crew manically juggled applicants, assuring them that their time was coming, rescheduled appointments, and selectively answered the phones, all so they could manually examine each and every file in their possession. Some of those files were piled high around the perimeter of their small conference room—Merry Terry refused to let them hire a temp for a week so they could catch up with filing. *"It's not in the budget,"* she'd shriek whenever the subject was raised.

No file materialized with his name on it despite their best efforts. They found evidence of mouse droppings sprinkled into some of the folders, but none of the house mice, who were stubbornly hiding, answered to the name "Gutierrez."

"Are we going to lose our jobs?" asked Arielle.

The file turned up two hours later. On Merry Terry's secretary's desk. She had pulled it when the police called that morning to say that Geraldo had eighty-sixed his domestic partner of two years. Not the fault of Employment, but tell that to Merry Terry or to Melie's cramping insides.

The thing about Merry Terry was that while the movie, *Critters*, might be on prime TV one night, Merry Terry was on at Axis Mundi five days a week. Like the giant critter in the film, she was shaped like a furry bowling ball and could (and would) move swiftly down an aisle, knocking pins or people out of her way into the gutter to reach her goal.

Any time she rolled into Reception, all extraneous movement or conversation ceased on the instant. Red Alert! Pulses sped up, penises were said to retract, hair stood at attention on the napes of necks in the immediate vicinity. Breathing became shallow and a few were heard gasping for air.

Melie prepared herself by assuming the blankest look at her command and backing toward a wall, any wall. She went to enormous lengths to maintain at least four feet between her and Merry Terry at all times. She was going to have to tell her about Dr. Needles' choking of Babs, though. And soon. But not on her first day back.

The word on the street was that Merry Terry's sexual appetites veered toward the kinky—picking up runaways in bars, bringing them home to husband, dinner and bed. Melie could not bear to think about any sexual act involving Merry Terry—her own neck started to itch whenever she did. She had noticed, however, that Merry Terry favored quasi-intimate têtes-à-têtes, leaning over Melie (and other women in the department) and touching their arms, shoulders, hair.

Critters were little engines of destruction and mayhem that could roll themselves together into one enormous ball and barrel past their human pursuers. Many wound up splattered all over the set when the Good Guys triumphed. With Merry Terry, that outcome did not seem likely, though one never knew. In the meantime Melie and crew had to live with her.

Merry Terry rolled in again, flaring her nostrils, sniffing and snorting. Melie had dressed in haste that morning. She glanced down at her black linen shirt and black pants with thin *red* stripes—what a tactical error.

Merry Terry sighted her, tossed her head and flared her nostrils, trampling everything in her path on the way to Melie. "Why," she demanded, "is Keisha Anne Woods, an aide, making an appointment to see me?"

Melie shook her head and put up her hands. "I don't know her."

"I'm seeing her at two PM."

Melie said nothing.

"You know I don't want to see employees—that's your job." She poked her finger toward Melie's abdomen, pivoted on her stubby toes, and charged out of the room.

"What was that about?" Geena asked, entering Melie's office with her eyes popping. "You could hear that out in Reception."

"Oh nothing," Melie replied, surveying her stack of pink messages. "Time to start the day. Keisha Anne Woods—isn't that Dr. Tamis' aide in OB-GYN? His name seems to be coming up a lot today."

At last, after a choked-down lunch and a brief afternoon walk, Melie had an administrator to deal with.

"You know what, Deedee, just send her home." Melie dabbed at her face with a tissue, wondering why the heat was turned up so high.

"I can do that?"

"Yes, she's violating the dress code. You're the dermatology department administrator. You told her to wear a lab coat."

Will this day never end?

"Yeah, she's a floozy with those cheeky little breasts of hers always peeking out of her necklines and those miniskirts . . ."

I have to concentrate, Melie told herself, noting that DeeDee had no figure of her own to speak of.

"Dee, wait—is it true you told the rest of the staff she had been on welfare?"

"Oh, everybody knows that," Deedee said calmly, sitting back in her chair, holding out one hand, admiring her new manicure.

"They do now. And about her mother's affair with the caseworker?"

Dee's head snapped around. "What about it?"

"Wasn't that told to you in confidence?"

"Look, Melie, I take these girls in off the street and give them careers in healthcare. If they're smart and they listen to me. But they're a bunch of tramps."

"Dee—oh, never mind. Maybe next time you should look to hire someone a bit more mature?"

"Older? Nah! I like 'em young so I can mold them right."

Melie took a deep breath. She walked her to the door and opened it. "Write it up as a written warning, Dee, and show me the draft first."

That evening, home at last, Melie followed her nighttime ritual: eating her plain Greek yogurt and cornflakes in bed with Furryface, her black and white cat, snuggling close. She would let the phone ring if it rang. She might scream if she heard another problem and who could resist telling her one?

She grabbed her notebook and spent half an hour trying to rewrite a poem. *I could write like this every day, every moment, and never stop and become completely asocial, mute, trapped inside my own linguistic mazes, a befuddled minotaur (minus Theseus in slow and meticulous pursuit). I could never talk to another living soul again, just play forever, in my mind.*

So inviting.

Could be dangerous, she thought. Very. She turned off the light and wondered—would she ever again be touched by human hands?

Melie was on a date. The guy was beefy, gruff, imposing. They were looking at French art and antiques through a store window. He knew what was what. She, though her major was French, identified many wrong. She made mistakes and felt humiliated.

He picked her up in her old apartment. She took a long time closing up the apartment, finding the cat. She had trouble getting out of the house.

She and her date were next seen observing another couple on a date, amused that the guy was telling the girl he loved her and the girl believed him. The girl was a French silk factory worker and the man had money. He bought silk rugs without asking her advice. She learned he was married.

Melie's date confessed, "I never say 'I love you.' Cheapened word." She told him kids use the word constantly. Neighbor's kid always asks her if she loves him. Her date was not impressed. He used, threw French words at her.

She was wary but not really. Sucking up as always. Taken in. Did she even like him? She didn't ask herself. She was simply grateful to be there. And he gave no reading of whether he liked her.

He wanted to buy a mask for six francs. They were eating at a sidewalk café. He hinted she should lend him money until he could use his cash card.

She was trying hard on this date to be amenable and adaptable and spontaneous and flexible—until she saw the buttons on his lap! The third or fourth button could create a sound that would pitch the body for complete submission.

Melie woke up in a flash, whimpering, "Someone please save me!" Even her dream dates ended badly. Or was this a good ending? She guessed maybe a shrink could tell her, if she still had a shrink.

CHAPTER II
SEEDS OF THE MELTDOWN

Melie dully watched the stations tick by as she rode the train into the city the next morning. No more daydreaming about PTM, his manly build, his bespoke suits, his sun-streaked hair; no more hopes of his rescuing her from her dreary life.

All about her, as far as her eyes could see, the morning's troop of flatliners were deciding whether to restore sinus rhythm or go the other way.

She glanced around the train, chasing a glimmer of motion, a routine from countless mornings, a way of folding the paper, snapping the attaché case closed, picking at the nose. She did not want to panic. Enough time for that once she got to the office. She recognized none of the expressionless faces and felt her heart start to stutter. Had she warped into a *Twilight Zone* rerun?

Everyone was gone. Maybe she had landed in an alternative universe or been shifted to a fourth dimension or the pod people had finally munched their way through the brains of all the other commuters.

They looked human. Well, maybe not. She must keep calm like Kevin McCarthy in *Invasion of the Body Snatchers*, who had kept himself safe while truckloads of giant pods (shaped like the cockroach eggs she found under her sink) whizzed by on the interstate and his very own girlfriend transformed before his eyes into an extraterrestrial and a bad kisser.

Just as she was locating the emergency brake, a tall, fashionably dressed, well-built man cat-walked down the aisle. She followed his every movement, especially the greasy blond hair, tied back with a red rubber band as it bounced on the nape of his neck. Oh, dear. For over a year she'd fantasized about their relationship, the intimacies they'd shared, how, for one brief second, their souls leapt out, danced ring-around-the-rosy, high-jumped in the air. Sigh.

Bulletin from Melie to World: Pony Tail Man restores order. About time. PTM, her one-time love. Dream Boy. Stalkee. Sleazeball. Still sexy? Yup.

He walked on by, never glancing in her direction.

Sigh.

She would like someone someday to know the care she'd taken with her clothes and makeup in case she ran into him on the train or platform. Her staff teased her about interviewing somewhere else. No such luck. But she knew she had to layer rolls and rolls of thick durable wallpaper over spots in her life like this one—little moments of madness—and walk amongst the living in the bright light of day. Undiscovered. Unfortunately, not invulnerable.

If we're ever surrounded by peapod people, PTM and me, at least I'm a good kisser! Not that I'm getting much practice. A wry smile crossed Melie's lips as she muttered to herself and stared out at the tall brown project buildings, empty sandlots, mothers walking their backpacked daughters to the entrance of the local public school.

She stood to put on her coat, her old cashmere one, noticing again the small hole in the shoulder where her shoulder bag strap wore through the material. She jockeyed for position near the door. She still had not had a date in four years, this morning's fantasies and last night's oneiric adventures notwithstanding.

Nothing had changed. For the last leg of the trip, the train wended its agonizingly slow way through the tunnel. Half the commuters still lined up, gray, pinched; half still remained seated until the last minute, grabbing when the train pulled in for genitals and briefcases. All, with their dented styrofoam cups of coffee sludge and smudgy newspapers, poking into her with their elbows and knees, squeezing past her into the narrow opening, invariably leaving her behind, gasping for breath.

There might not be enough air one day when this happened. She had to fight to get out, rise to the surface. She paddled blindly, more than a little frantic. Still . . .

14

Nothing was changed. Nothing does change overnight, she thought. Wasn't that the basis of therapy and millions of therapists' choices of vacations, boats, tennis camps and private schools?

But wait—something had changed. *My dream man's a slug!*

Melie Kohl was running late to work. Again. She pictured her boss at this very moment, thrumming her stubby fingers on top of the Reception desk, waiting. The poor job seekers filling out their applications, trying to get the dates from the résumé in their hands to match the dates they were filling in on the sheets, trying desperately to rehearse, to keep their stories straight, had to encounter her bull-like glare whenever they lifted their heads for air.

Melie needed to get off the train now and run like hell for the subway. Then run like hell for the crosstown bus. Then walk in with a story. *Oh, damndamndamn!*

Ten minutes late, Melie nodded to Merry Terry, who would just have to wait, ushered her first supplicant into the office, and closed the door. It was none other than the dashing Dr. Tamis, Axis Mundi's gentleman doctor from Georgia, head of obstetrics and gynecology, who had gotten wind that some sort of a complaint was about to be lodged against him.

Arielle buzzed her on the intercom. "Dean Terry wants to see you out here pronto."

Melie excused herself and joined Merry Terry for a huddle at the Reception desk. "Listen here," Merry Terry whispered in her ear, "according to that Woods woman I met with yesterday, Dr. Tamis did . . .stuff . . .acted inappropriately. Find out if it's true."

"But . . ."

Merry Terry had already charged out of Reception back to her office down the hall.

Melie sat down behind her desk again, facing the tall strapping man from Georgia. She let him ramble on for a few minutes, and then she carefully explained that rubbing one's hand—repeatedly— over a chosen employee's bent-over buttocks, even if performed with the most altruistic of motives, was not within the parameters of Axis Mundi Medical Center's policy or procedure.

"Why don't I just show you what I did?" suggested Dr. Tamis, as he stood up and started circling around the desk toward Melie.

She threw him a look that she hoped like hell was "askance" and waved him down. "No," she said calmly, "that's quite all right. Just tell me in words."

She wondered. Would he have grasped her by the back of the neck, pulled her roughly toward him, and kissed her passionately, his tongue slipping insidiously between her teeth? Or given her only the polite good-bye peck on the cheek, the same he claimed to have administered to his aide? She reached for a Kleenex and patted her face dry.

The doctor shrugged. "Do you mind explaining to me what sexual harassment is exactly, Melie?"

She did her best: words, looks, pictures, gestures, molestation, anything uncomfortable, threatening, hostile—as perceived by the victim.

"You know how it is. It's hard for GYN's sometimes to draw the line."

She took a minute to ponder this admission, and then asked, "How do you mean, Dr. Tamis?"

Dr. Tamis cleared his throat. "Our patients come in very upset . . ."

She swallowed the bile rising in her throat and said, "Keisha Anne Woods is not a patient."

"Staff too." He looked wistfully out the window for a moment. Melie thought she saw a smirk on his face.

"I see."

Melie took another moment to wonder about Tamis' brand of Southern comfort. She'd better connect with Keisha Anne Woods, his administrative aide, very soon, and, dare she say, probe a little deeper? Dr. Tamis launched into a version of events with the emphasis on his "fatherly concern" and "compassionate" behavior.

Geez, Melie thought, *I've only been gone one frigging week!*

After ten years of Axis Mundi, Melie was reaching a point, at some particularly bad moments, when she thought she might go stark raving mad. The good news would be that she would no longer be responsible, that people would have to take care of her. The good news was she would learn the secret of all those nogoodnik, lazy, obligations-shirking, substance-snorting "problem employees." The good news was that she'd have a rest, though maybe a final one. The good news was that she wouldn't have to smile, pass hankies, and say, "I see," with a perfectly modulated voice, punctuated by a nonjudgmental nod. The bad news was that she couldn't think of any at moments like these.

She supposed her breakdown could take several forms. Much like those babies left in a damp bassinet in an isolated wing of the orphanage, Melie sometimes felt she would shrivel up and literally die if she weren't "handled" in the coming twenty-four hours. She constructed an elaborate solution—she would stand on a street corner in the Village and solicit bodily contact. With her natural instincts for such things, however, she was sure that at the twenty-third hour, she would accompany a distraught woman to a coffee shop, a woman who just had to tell her the trouble she was in.

In another scenario, Melie would stop dead center in Grand Central Station and cause a pileup of commuter bodies, already more than half dead, exceeding the capacity of neighborhood medical centers. The homeless would have to be kicked off their benches to make room for fallen commuters. The station would turn into a big ER. Eventually, commuters would be sent home to their suburban tracts with body lice and fleas—they too deserved a trip to the country once in a while.

In any case, a Melie Meltdown was coming—she could hear the rumbling. She'd already sought out the unused restrooms in the basement a couple of times, closing herself into a stall to shriek, "Where is my life?" and "I'm a person too!"

How did she wind up in this racket? Like liberal arts majors everywhere, she had cast about for a way to earn a living. Her generally affable manner, pleasant looks, surface imperturbability had landed her in HR. *What a racket*, she had thought initially. To be paid just for listening to people? Granted she had to "arrange" things for them occasionally—how hard could that be?

That was before she learned about the psychological weight of last-minute rescue missions, life and death decisions regarding employees' livelihoods, tyrannical bosses, facing down overly credentialed, entitled, mostly infantile doctors, even defending some in human right commission hearings . . . before she realized her social life had gone out the window. . . before she withdrew to a place where none could touch her.

Where was her life?

After Tamis left, Melie reminded herself to schedule Keisha Anne Woods for later that week. Then she happened to look down at her hands. She counted four bitten, almost bloody, cuticles. No kidding. Her post-vacation reentry wasn't proving easy.

Last week, deciding she needed to do something brave for her birthday, she'd taken the whole week off and spent it mostly renting talky French films from her local video store and taking the neighbor's boy out for an ice cream. When Friday rolled around, however, she'd rented a car and gone upstate to Finn Lake on a Lonelyhearts singles ski weekend. The cross-country skiing amazed her. A lesson or two and she felt she had mastered the techniques. She loved that no matter what mistakes she made, she wouldn't have too far to fall. But though the skiing was exhilarating, she'd had to find a way to escape her fellow skiers who persisted in trying to get to know her. She took to her car and drove around aimlessly, finally stopping in front of a barn with a crooked sign which read: YE OLDE ANTIQUE SHOPPE.

She entered the cavernous space, and as she always did, looked around quickly to get her bearings and discover her degree of vulnerability. She fell into this room though, and stood dazzled by the space: generous, with many deep recesses, ledges, corridors leading nowhere, unexpected culs de sac, corners with tricky accesses and uncertain exits.

Everywhere were rusted farm implements, Grandpa's old pitchforks, Grandma's embroidered aprons, Daddy's three-wheeler, cradles, penny-books, armoires, chamber pots, rolltop desks, Depression china, parts of someone's tea set, moth-eaten quilts, pillows, beaten-up porcelain dolls, ankle-length cotton skirts, chess sets, and records. She noticed a wooden box with green marbles inside, resting on a doily atop a comic book in a basin on an oak table with a cracked mirror—layers and layers of life.

Caught off guard, Melie felt uncentered. Before she could retreat, the owner seized upon his customer, chatting her up mercilessly.

He's got me in his beak like a bird of prey, and he's not letting go until he's good and ready, Melie realized. Was he lonely? She regarded him carefully and decided to listen. He was falling headlong, as they always did, into her social worker's face with his entire life story: how he dropped out of school, had to sell textbooks for a living, rarely saw his kids after his wife ran off with another man, his wife who had detested country living.

He was a man about a decade older than her, she guessed. Average looks. Maybe a little better than average: tall with a mop of thick hair, strong build, open face. She really liked the grey-white-red brush of a beard on his chin. The red really fascinated her, how it grew there in the middle, like a poppy in a bank of day-old snow. She had longed to stroke that chin with her index finger, smooth those bristles. She spent over an hour talking to him, admiring his photographs, wondering: *Does he like me? Could he be made to like me?* He really was decent looking, and his store had an aura of mystery.

His companion, though, gave her pause. Gladys. A big red parrot with yellow, green and blue markings, beady eyes and sharpened beak. From its filthy cage, it seemed to eye her with a good degree of malevolence, as if threatening, "Lose an eye! Lose an ear!"

She decided not to get any closer. She made an excuse that others were waiting for her back at the inn. He folded up his photo album and tucked it under the counter in a hidden place.

"Do you ever get up in these parts?"

"Not really." *Why?*

"Lady, look me up if you do."

She took the business card he held out to her. Ted Baer, Antiquaire.

"All right." She felt obliged to give him one of her own. She grabbed a small green perfume bottle, which he seemed almost reluctant to sell her, and made to leave. At the front door she turned and secretly watched as the man, Ted, poured himself some coffee and regained his post on the stool behind the counter. She saw him pivot and pin her business card to the Xanadu Insurance Company calendar behind his head. He scratched the back of his head and took a sip of the hot comforting liquid. That's when she overheard him say, "Hey, Gladys, what did you think?"

That night in the lounge at the Finn Lake B&B, Melie sat in the overly warm room, sipping dark beer, sucking the salt off beer nuts, while listening to a lanky guitarist singing her favorite songs about crashes on the levee, eves of destruction, the day the music stopped. She watched the town vet/night hour musician, his impossibly long thin legs in blue jeans stretched out before him, and noticed how his bristly thick handlebar mustache, color of honey and sand, rose and quivered above the steel harmonica braced against his skin.

Someone else would know how to take advantage of a situation like this.

Then her mind returned to the antique dealer. How did he get that bit of red smack in the middle of his goatee? What was that all about? And that evil bird. . .

The rest of the workday passed in a blur. Getting ready for bed that night, Melie considered the red bird, so at home, *l'oiseau de l'antiquaire.* Squatting on its bar in front of its filthy steel cage, looking out on a vista of blackened, cracked, and broken seeds, spread out in a semicircle below, its handiwork of the last week, thinking contentedly, *I done good,* thinking, *I'm gonna scare that New York City bitch away,* its thinking punctuated by its darting evil parrot eyes and jagged bone white parrot beak.

Not such a formidable rival, really. Could whine a bit in its fashion, she imagined, be a general nuisance, pierce the outer skin with that beak, screech, jump up and down in place, pout in its cage, pull a face at her, hate her.

But it would be so out in the open. She could take it for what it was. Surely. And she'd never have to give it a hug. Or solve its problems. Just maybe once in a while some strokes, some finger scratching behind the ears.

Melie thought of the man too: The man's eyes had been kind, she thought; his talk, lonely. He had liked sharing his photos of beavers, deer, and loons on the lake. She suspected he longed in his way for a change from parrot company, another companion paddling the canoe while he took moving shots, a reason to close the Shoppe early, or take a trip to see his kids, or a hunting expedition further north for green perfume bottles in an attic, wooden secretaries, cigar boxes, phonographs that scratched old-time music and comedy routines out of what he told her were Edison Blue Amberol cylinder records.

She would write him a postcard, now. *I'd like to hear more about loons on the lake . . .* Or at lunch tomorrow. Or no, in bed later, propped over her nightly bowl of white goop. What harm could come of this? He had liked her. She sensed it and her senses were never wrong.

Every few days Melie had a regular visitor.

"You have an aura about you," said Babs the Chokee, during one of their impromptu meetings. She stared at something just north of Melie's left eyebrow.

"Aura or odor?"

Babs grabbed her right hand, stilling the drumming. "And you never seem to get ruffled."

Melie heard this a lot: "You're so calm." She also heard: "You have the worst job at Axis Mundi Medical Center." To which she responded silently: *I do, don't I?*

Melie slid her hand out of the other's grasp. "Let's get back to you, shall we?"

Babs stuck out her tongue.

Now I'm dealing with two-year-olds. "Has the pinching stopped?"

"The choking? Mostly. She started in again this morning so I grabbed my bag and came running over here."

"I see. Look, I'm working on your situation."

"Whatever. Melie, I've been thinking. This is not meant for you—this is not your life!

"Uh..."

"But hurry, Melie!" Babs said, gathering up her things and heading out the office door.

Melie closed her eyes for a moment after Babs left. She was having trouble focusing on what she needed to do. Sukie knocked on her door and entered. "I have to tell you something."

"Sit."

"Keisha Anne Woods came to see me while you were in with Tamis. I hired her, you see, and placed her first with DeeDee. But she's what you'd call a provocative dresser. And streetwise. DeeDee was going to fire her for talking back and being sassy. I saved Keisha Anne Woods by moving her over to OB-GYN."

Melie mentally rolled her eyes. "What's she saying now, Sukie?"

"Keisha Anne Woods says that Tamis is rubbing himself against her in the records room, leaning over her when she's typing, maybe touching her ass once, but that could have been an accident. She says she tried telling him to cut it out, but he doesn't get it." Sukie paused. "I can't believe what she's saying, Mel. He's so fine."

Matches my perception of Tamis though. "Anything else, Sukie?"

"Even though I brought her in, I have to say that she's not reliable. Not a solid citizen. I seem to remember that she brought a similar complaint against a woman supervisor at her previous employment."

Melie nodded thoughtfully. "So how did you end it with her?"

"I told her, 'Run away little girl!'"

"No? Sukie!"

Sukie shook her head proudly. "Everyone's in awe of Dr. Tamis and his scientific contributions. We can't let a little twerp like her blemish his standing here."

"Go now, Sukie."

Note to self: Bring Merry Terry up to speed. She's not going to want to hear this. She's as much in awe of Tamis as everyone else. The whole Center. She will be merciless—with me. I can't stall much more though. Anyone else but Tamis and I would have started the grievance process already.

And let's not forget Babs, my new best girlfriend, and Dr. Needles. Physical abuse. This is huge. I'm just going to transfer her out somewhere, get her out of harm's way. I don't want to deal with Merry Terry on this too.

Do your job, Melie!

CHAPTER III

SEEDS STARTING TO SPROUT

First week back, Melie had somehow made it to Friday afternoon and was experiencing a lull, the kind only December brings. As much as she disliked having things sprung on her, she'd been programmed to jump from crisis to crisis to crisis. Empty time bred strange monsters.

She stared at her phone. Not chirping. Nothing interesting was going on outside her window. Merry Terry had taken a rare day off. Melie's mind wandered.

She had never had much luck in the romance department. She had mostly wandered in unawares while shopping for other things—a new used car, a kitten, another bored girl to go to the movies with.

Once she had answered an ad in a Personals column. It was a poem really. She had dated the guy for about a month. She thought it was going all right, but she didn't have much to compare it to. They had sex, of course, which left her curiously overstimulated, antsy, feeling no feeling. Still she had liked the idea that she had a boyfriend. She even tried to talk to him, interest him in herself.

After a few weeks though, he decided that he preferred to play the field. "After all, it's like I'm in this big candy store." He admitted he hadn't written the poem either. He told her he had copied it out of a romance novel and was surprised anyone would fall for such mush.

Melie's other adventures had the same sort of ring to them. Her longest relationship, six whole months, she'd had with a lawyer. Four years ago. Ending badly. Men seemed to want something she just couldn't give.

They drifted in and out, leaving more rusted wreckage in her dump of a heart. She looked for patterns. She saw she was too flattered and grateful when they asked her out. She worked too hard at getting that elusive second date. She rarely asked herself if this was the man she wanted.

She often thought a French lover would do fine with her. She had spent six weeks in a little town in Normandy when she was a junior in college. She had seen enough to know the French preferred going to the cinema, drinking *café crème*, and discussing politics to confessing anything ever to anyone.

From boyfriends she had learned that though she had been hanging on to her thirties by a thread, she still had a slim sexy body that they liked to fondle, mash, and kiss. They were usually amazed that that body lay beneath her clothes (so colorless, so tailored), and suggested she might want to dress a little more provocatively. But Melie didn't relish the idea of anyone at Axis Mundi fondling, mashing or kissing her body, so she kept things as they were.

Was coffee a chemical? Melie choked down the last mouthful, cold and gritty, then deposited the bitten Styrofoam cup in the "round file." She shuffled the five pink slips on her desk. *I shouldn't buy from that coffee vendor on the corner—what was I thinking? Where does he get his water from, anyway?* She bit her lip. A quick glance at the compact mirror—thank God she hadn't broken the skin.

Soon to be 3:00 PM, witching hour in HR. Dr. Tamis; Keisha Anne Woods; Babs, her dentist; Dining Room Jim—which to tackle first? If she could only make it through the next couple of hours . . .

The buzz of the intercom rattled through Melie's head like the dreaded sound of her dentist's drill. Arielle announced, "Melie, it's Jim again. He called before when you were down the hall."

"I know."

"He says he has a little problem."

"Arielle, he never has little problems."

"Jim, what's up?"

"Mel, that cook I hired two months ago? He's on his way over to your office." Jim's voice cracked.

"O—kay. What am I supposed to do with him? This isn't the Principal's Office, you know."

"Oh, you're funny. I just fired him. He's on probation still. I . . . I didn't like his attitude."

"Guess he couldn't take your bullying?" Melie ventured. "Great." (Pause) "I'll exit him, but will you please try to give me some notice next time?"

She hung up the phone and buzzed Arielle on the intercom. "Arielle, expect one unhappy camper coming up from Dining Hall." She started to make a quick call to Dr. Wong to confirm her appointment for a root canal the next day when she was interrupted by Arielle. Jim again.

"Mel, I just wanted to tell you that this guy's a bit angry . . ."

"Hmm," Melie hung up and got back on with her dentist's office. The intercom buzzed again.

"And—he's got his knives with him."

"His . . . knives?

"He's a cook, remember? His knives are in his bag."

3:30 PM, and according to Arielle, the cook had arrived, slamming the door, and was pacing back and forth in the Reception area, unnerving the other occupants: a toothless transfer candidate, an applicant taking a typing test, and another pressed against the wall, stepping out of the woolen slacks she wore under her dress.

Melie propped her Timex up on her desk. She pressed the panic button dangling from a cord around her neck to summon Security.

3:45 PM: Arielle came into Melie's office, frowning. "I dunno . . . this guy's making me nervous. Where's Security?"

"Give it a few more minutes," said Melie, biting her lower lip. *Where the hell is Security?*

Geena bounced in. "What going on?" Melie shooed her away.

"Stay in your office," Melie barked.

Geena's hands rose to the sides of her face, her mouth opened wide. "Oooh." A perfect parody of *The Scream*.

4:01 PM: Arielle let her know the cook was getting more and more agitated. Melie knew she could stall no longer.

She was wearing her straight black wool dress with all the zippers at

25

the wrists and from midsection up to her throat. She felt reasonably safe. She had not forgotten to put on her lip seal this morning either.

She girded her loins and strode into Reception, easily spotting her exit interview candidate, the cook whom she had never met before: a rough-looking character in a tee shirt. Taking a deep breath, she forced herself to extend her hand. He took it in his vise-like grip and shook vigorously, putting on display muscled forearms pitted with scars and tattoos. Forcing a smile, Melie showed him into Geena's office, which opened right off the Reception area and seemed safer than her own back office.

"You can leave your bag on the sofa," she instructed.

He obediently put the heavy bag down.

Geena sat behind her desk, the cook near the door at the tiny conference table, Melie across from him against the back wall. *Crikes, Melie* thought, *never back yourself into a corner with a disgruntled employee! At least that's what they said at last month's "Preventing Violence in Today's Workplace, a one-day workshop for HR professionals." Too late now!*

"I understand this is your last day, Derrick. Can you tell me what's been going on?"

As Derrick described what a frigging tyrant Jim was, she focused on providing the ultimate in compassion and understanding, careful not to validate his bad behavior in any way. She made sure to keep her voice steady when she asked, "Derrick, is it true you threatened to poison the salad bar?"

Silence. He looked sheepish for a moment then shot up out of his seat, gesticulating wildly. "You don't know what that little guy does to you, how he makes you feel—"

"I understand," Melie broke in, "but you know we can't keep you on after a threat like that."

Derrick crumbled then, falling back into his seat and putting his head in his hands. Melie shot a look at Geena who passed the tissues. Derrick grabbed a wad and Melie felt she could stop holding her breath now. Maybe because she did intend to go through with her root canal, God was being kind to her. Situation defused, right? *Boy, am I good.*

Melie was winding up the exit interview, telling him when to expect his last check, how to apply for unemployment benefits, where to seek medical coverage, all while moving toward the office door. Without a word of warning the cook bounded up and darted out of the office. Melie and Geena exchanged a quick frightened look, but before they had time to act, he had returned and plunked his bag (with the knives) down on the conference table. He started unzippering it.

Melie flew past him out of the room, guiltily leaving Geena trapped behind her desk. Peering back into the room, Melie saw him take out several lethal-looking specimens, sharp as shark teeth, and line them up on the table. He held them up, one by one, and seemed to be fingering them. *What do I do now?*

She walked back into the room, assuming what she hoped was a stern and professional demeanor. Squaring her narrow shoulders, drawing herself up to her full sixty-two inches, she declared, "It's time for you to go now, Derrick."

The cook hesitated and looked a bit lost. He had a long knife in his hand and was running his fingers absentmindedly along its cutting edge.

"You'll be happier somewhere else," she stammered. "Away from Jim."

He looked Melie up and down and shrugged. She and Geena watched as he lifted the tools of his trade, one by one, off the table, and lovingly placed them back in his bag. When there was one knife left, he stepped back on one leg and lunged forward in Melie's direction, making a little Z flourish in the space between them. Then he packed that knife up too, folded in the unemployment and benefits papers, zippered up the bag, and stood rock still.

Gulping, Melie gestured toward the door. "Bye now," she squeaked. She clumsily pantomimed his walking out the door.

Derrick squinted at her, then at Geena, shaking his head as if to say, *What pitiful creatures.* He nodded once, a bitter nod. Then he was gone.

Geena looked a little less oblivious than usual. She ran to the ladies' room, most likely to put on some rouge, Melie guessed, and maybe to up-chuck a little. Arielle, at the front desk, had morphed into a *Ghostbusters* extra; she had witnessed the Zorro bit. Sukie, luckily, had been out of the office for some remedial training on the new computers Merry Terry had installed. She would surely have thrown lighter fuel into the action or selflessly sacrificed herself upon the altar for the sake of Axis Mundi.

Melie crawled back to her office to collapse, resting her head on her desk. A half-hour later Security showed up, two punky kids claiming they had been roaming around the building—*as if there's anyone at Axis Mundi who doesn't know how to find the Principal's Office!*

When she was sufficiently recovered, Melie made her last executive decision of the day: no way would she return the other three calls. She left at 4:50 PM on the dot—Merry Terry let them leave early only on Christmas Eve—and zombie-walked to the train, whimpering quietly to herself.

Rush hour resembled another dream she had had, no, more a meditative trance, of a prehistoric her squatted down on her haunches, watching the bison roar past. Only this was more terrible.

Panic rose in bubbles in her throat. She felt she couldn't breathe— though of course she could, she reminded herself. But she yanked at her turtleneck to let some air in.

She wobbled, and lost all but a tunnel of vision. All she heard was the *thwack thwack thwack* of marching shoeshined loafers, menacing clicks of high-priced heels, sharpened hipbones colliding, occasional fat rumps bumping.

As she halted dead in the middle of rush hour at Grand Central Station, the herds obligingly parted around her, snarling and pushing, rushing mindlessly, or of one mind, toward their destiny.

She scissored sideways through the herd. She needed to find a wall, for safety. How observe them, know where she was, if she was stuck in the middle? She cast about like some small animal drowning unnoticed in a neighborhood creek. The herd gave no sign of letting up. She had to make a move soon. She couldn't stand being exposed like this . . .

Soon she was resting inches from a wall, careful not to touch it, feeling protected by its dirty blankness, its unpeopled surface behind her. The herd moved on without her.

A filthy homeless man with ropes of dreadlocked hair held forth his dented paper cup, mumbling "Help" at her, keeping his balance while holding on to a dozen plastic bags filled with unknown smelly crap, his valuables. She drew back against the wall, clutching her briefcase, her own plastic bags, and herself.

To her rescue came a 350-pound train conductor, approaching on her right, only marginally less terrifying. She gulped for air and waited to see what he would do to her.

He walked between her and the homeless man, not glancing at either. He just fit, just squeezed by. Another few inches or pounds and he wouldn't have made it. Melie guessed he knew that. She watched him get on line for popcorn. Popcorn was sort of a diet food, wasn't it?

She remembered the homeless man closing in and turned, only to find him down the road apiece, taking change from the hands of a sweet young thing who did not appear to be sweating or gulping or to be bothered in the least.

Melie forged ahead through the gate to her train. She definitely was going to insist on an aisle seat tonight.

Hardly surprising: Sunday night and Melie was having a time getting to sleep. *Don't think about the work week,* she commanded herself. Her subconscious had other plans as she discovered when she finally drifted off.

> She was standing on a subway platform. A menacing man appeared next to her and without warning punched a button on his palm, and she flew upwards, her body flattened and hanging on a post. There was no one around to rescue her. Was this where she was going to die? Before she'd had a chance to live?

She awoke in a cold sweat and quickly relit the night table lamp. Too jumpy to sleep, she dug under the bed for her journal. She needed to think about something else, to get her mind off the dream. But she was soon off on another tangent.

> What are you going to do, girl? You can't remember the touch of human hands. And I suppose you're thinking you will just die if something doesn't happen in the next twenty-four hours?
>
> Maybe you slip on a white lace garter (with a little rose in the middle) over fishnet stockings (with a hole in one thigh), slide into killer stilettos, fold a leopardskin miniskirt around your slim hips, shimmy into a flesh tone

camisole, paint your fingernails, toes and mouth fire engine red? Swing a patent leather bag from your shoulder? Then saunter to the nearest lamppost in the light rain and wait for Bogey to sidle by in tan trenchcoat and say, "Going my way?"

(Cue KT Oslin singing, "What's a woman to do. . .")

No, you stare at the blank page: the horror, the horror. Rich widows could hire a gigolo—but you're not getting rich off an Axis Mundi salary and you don't hang out in the right places (Riviera?) or any places, for that matter. Young women can hook up with friends for what in your college days was called a mercy fuck. Or go to bars. But women your age? Jewish singles events? Shudder. Singles hiking? Not working.

How soon do "things" atrophy? Ask Dr. Tamis—he'll know (snicker).
Melie slammed the journal shut, jumped up, spilling Furryface off the side of the bed, and made for her usual cure: a shot glass half full of cognac. She downed it in one gulp though it burned a discrete hole in her stomach lining.
Back in bed, she wrote:

I followed the guy with straight blond hair falling in his face back to his place. He was weaving all over the sidewalk and I tried to guide him, but I wasn't doing too much better. Up five flights and into a tiny studio we went. I turned on a light while he flopped onto his mattress on the floor, rummaging around in a corner. I sat down beside him and took the joint he offered me. "Undress?" he asked, and we each took off our own clothes. He put out the joint carefully in an ashtray on the floor, sighed, and rolled over on top of me. Nothing stirred. . . I wrapped my legs around his hips and pumped. Not even a mouse. I rubbed his cute little butt. When that didn't work either, I started kissing his nipples. Then I thought I heard a sob.

He rolled off me and said, "This is too much work."

"Work?" I repeated. (Was there a gun somewhere nearby?)

"I don't . . .girls don't . . .I sometimes . . ."

"You're. . .gay? That's it, right?"

"No. If anything, a little bi."

A little bi? I thought on the cab ride home. A little bi, but he can't stop crying over Todd, his best bud who died at Mercy over a year ago. I listened to the whole story—who could resist telling me? Oh, he'd had lots of girls too, lots.

By the end of the week, I could think of it without crying.

Melie slid the journal back under the bed and flicked off the light. She stretched out on her stomach. She was soon joined by Furryface who settled in on the backs of her legs. Lifting her head, she asked the cat, "What would you do if you were me?" Furryface blinked. Silly Melie. Furryface was a fat lap cat and "fixed." She could hardly be expected to empathize. Within seconds she was emitting tranquil and rhythmic kitty snores.

Three more hours and it would be time to start a new day, catch a train. She climbed out of bed and headed for her closet, pulling out a brown wool sweater, black slacks, boxy black blazer and black boots with brown trim. She inspected everything, found no moth holes or pulls or scuffs, and laid the clothes on the rocking chair in the corner. She hated surprises, especially early morning when she'd had no sleep. She padded into the kitchen and put up a kettle of tea, sitting in the dark, propping up her head with her arm.

Four years and counting . . .

CHAPTER IV

BUT THESE WERE MERE CRISES...

Every problem in New York City seemed to find its way through the door of the Employment Office, sooner rather than later, confronting Melie across her big fat desk. December with its "joyous" vibe always brought out the most aberrant behavior.

9 AM

"Carla, tell me," Melie implored, putting on her best you-can-tell-me-anything face.

Carla was a sweet young black administrator Melie knew she could trust, as clueless as the rest of them, but smart enough to follow up on Melie's suggestions. *We should really have lunch sometime.*

"Is what I heard correct? You found candles?"

Carla nodded. "Yes. She was supposed to be cleaning up the file room her last week on the job. When we went in there Monday morning, the room was trashed, and there were candles burnt down everywhere."

"Like, how many?"

"Eight or nine."

"That's . . . a lot."

"Another thing. Whenever she had a dispute with a doctor or another secretary, she would give them this little doll and say, 'You'll need this.'"

"Wow. Like voodoo or something?"

Carla shrugged. "She really freaked out the other women in the office, let me tell you."

Melie pushed her damp hair off her forehead, picked up a pen, put it down. "You know, she's still asking me to rehire her. I'm a little afraid to tell her no. I said maybe to a less demanding job. But now . . ."

"Maybe you shouldn't."

"Yeah, maybe not."

Carla went to the office door, opened it a crack, and then shut it. She came back into the room. "One other thing, Melie."

Melie stopped her note taking and looked up expectantly.

"What I want to say is that one candle looked a bit like . . . you."

"Oh, c'mon, Carla. I can't believe—"

Carla nodded her head up and down vigorously.

"But why would she—"

"Melie, you're my friend so I can tell you: everyone hates HR."

10 AM

"You ever need your bathroom at home redone—or any touch-ups—here, take my card, Just call. I'll come right over." Paolo, the director of facilities, appeared to be winking.

Did he mean what she thought he meant? Melie nodded.

Paolo stood up tucking his white open-necked shirt into the back of his impossibly tight jeans. Was he a workout buff, Italian film star, garden variety lecher?

"Be seeing you soon, I hope!" Paolo added, as he stalked off like some giant bird of prey.

(Sukie insisted Paolo did a lot of "touch-ups" on the lumpy sofabed installed in his basement office.)

Melie heard a lot of activity on York Avenue and went to the window. Out on the corner, ten firemen were beating on the hood of a new black sports car. It no longer looked so new. She realized its alarm had been sounding most of the time Paolo was in her office and now smoke seemed to be billowing from underneath the hood.

Playing to a crowd of onlookers, most gathered at Axis Mundi's windows, one intrepid fireman rushed off to his truck and returned with a hand extinguisher. He proceeded to blanket the car hood in white sticky powder. Then all his buddies took turns banging on the hood with a mallet until the hood had peaks and valleys and was no longer smooth. At a certain mysterious moment, they appeared satisfied and left in a group. The fire trucks pulled out noisily.

Was this part of an ancient ritual? Maybe a Robert Bly invention. The firemen had not left a note. So naturally scores of Axis Mundians remained at their posts, hoping to catch sight of the car owner's expression when he returned—*wild guess*— from visiting his loud and obnoxious Aunt Tilly, who had just had her uterus taken out by Dr. Tamis.

Sure enough, just before noon, a portly, balding man returned to his sports car. He circled around it twice, wiped some of the white powder off the hood and just stood there shaking his head. Another man approached from the sidelines and speaking to him quietly, led him gently away. Melie saw the whole thing, stationed at her window, and her fervent reaction was: *Please don't bring him here!*

Almost Lunchtime?

Melie was free. Her stomach felt like thick rope coiled in a bucket in a corner of a boat, waiting to be let out. She did the only thing she knew. She walked down to the Benefits Office and poured herself another cup of Benefit, black, no sugar. She thought, lunch? Where could she eat today? Thai or Chinese? That new $5.95 spaghetti place?

"Melie, hi. Interested in getting a bite to eat?" asked a newly hired and very friendly administrator who was handing in her benefit enrollment forms.

"Can't make it today. Thanks." The thought of rapid-fire patter from her wannabe new pal plus the idea her pal might have some issues to discuss plus the idea that pal might not like walking one mile away just so Melie wouldn't run into anyone . . .

11:30 AM

She headed back to her office to grab her coat when Arielle buzzed her. "Franny's out here, crying and shaking."

Another one? The word evidently had gotten around that Melie was back at her post. "Send her in." She hung her coat up on the back of her door and assumed the position, her small frame half hidden behind her overlarge desk. Her raft. She wasn't coming off.

Franny walked in, glancing around nervously into all the nooks and crannies of the spacious office, littered with piles of multicolored paper, not unlike coral reefs, Melie thought, pebbles on the sand, white surf bubbles. If you used your imagination.

Franny located the tissue box deftly out of long habit and blew her nose before commencing. "My coworkers all hate me. I stand in the doorway and there's always someone saying something nasty about me, how I dress, how the patients don't like me—"

"Did you keep that appointment at EAP?"

"What?" Franny pulled a mirror out of her bag and rubbed at the smeared mascara under her eyes.

"The Employee Assistance Program. The appointment I made for you last week with the social worker?"

"Yes. Melie, they don't know anything over there. He said to make friends with the other secretaries, ask one out to lunch!"

"He did?"

"C'mon now. That's not how it happens in the real world."

Melie shook her head wearily. "Of course not."

"Just get me out of there. I need a transfer now. And don't tell me to look for a job elsewhere. I'm not leaving Axis Mundi. I like it here."

"Oh."

Noon

Melie walked in a huge circle for twenty minutes, getting a French vanilla bean frozen yogurt on the way back. Then she sat in the joint with the world's most terrific and strongest possible cup of caffeine. A highlight of her day.

1 PM

"Mel," Arielle called as soon as Melie walked in from lunch, "Dean Terry wants to see you in her office right away. About the Tamis investigation. She said to bring your notes. Oh—and plan to be with her for at least a couple of hours. But first the auditors want you to talk to Cherry Lum. She's waiting in your office."

Melie hurriedly hung up her coat and headed to her office. *Gotta love these ambushes.*

1:15 PM

"Cherry, there's $1,800 missing—we're still counting—in patient receipts—"

"So, why blame me? It's because I'm the only Asian in the department, right?"

"Excuse me, your initials are logged on the computer. You entered the changes but apparently never made the deposits." Melie smiled—she knew she had her there.

"*I'm going to the labor board!* I shoulda made a complaint long ago. My supervisor is a racist pig. Know what she said to the white girls when I was out getting coffee for them yesterday? 'When's that Chino coming back?'"

Melie swallowed. *Not another human rights case, please!* "Cherry, this is a serious allegation . . ."

2 PM

"Melie, you have to move this paragraph down here, see?

"Hmm."

"And change this to read this way." Merry Terry pointed, leaning in a bit closer.

"'We spoke to Dr. Tamis and she?'" Melie inquired calmly. She sat further back in her chair.

"Yes."

"But—"

"Let's not waste time."

They were at Revision #9 of the grievance decision—Ms. Woods had handed in a poorly-written grievance only two days before after days of innuendoes, stalling, threats, jockeying for position, calls from someone purporting to be her lawyer.

"Get it done by two o'clock tomorrow so I can show it to our attorney."

Melie knew that Merry Terry was eager to get the spotlight off Axis Mundi's star faculty member. "Terry, you do realize I don't have that much control of my schedule? I mean, just now, Cherry Lum . . . . It's the worst time of year for us in Employment. The crises keep on coming."

"I. Don't. Care. You can leave if you can't handle it . . . or are afraid!" Merry Terry lowered her face into Melie's and waited for the comeback.

"Right." Melie resisted all urges and sat there. At first. She willed herself to appear docile. Then realizing she did not have much to lose, she ventured, "Terry, on another matter, I think now that Geena and I are doing all the management training, our salaries should reflect this fact."

"*No more training!*" Merry Terry shot out of her seat and bellowed, shaking her head from side to side. Surely this had been heard through the thin office door.

Melie pushed on nevertheless. "How is it Lucille has training in her job description while we're the ones doing the training?"

Merry Terry ignored this last remark and launched into an impromptu review. "Speaking of job duties and performance, you're no good at employee relations.

"Whaaat?"

"You heard me." An evil smile lurked on her fat lips. "Your recruitment efforts have been adequate, I suppose."

"How can you say that?" Melie felt her heart playing skip rope with its beats.

"You're pretty good at filling the tech jobs, getting the science students in here."

Melie stood up. *"You don't even believe what you're saying!"* she shouted. She was sweating hard, white-faced and cramping.

Merry Terry smiled. "If you want to leave. . ."

Melie grabbed the grievance papers and beat it out the door. Heading outside, she made herself walk around the block five or six times until her breathing returned to normal.

3 PM – 5 PM

Back at her desk, returning phone calls, Melie issued a heretofore incalculable number of "I see's" to cover a) the drunken autopsy tech; b) the drunken housekeeper; c) the crazy psychiatrist ("My feelings were hurt"); d) the secretary who was convinced that her supervisor was poisoning her orange juice because she had seen her emptying a packet of something while spying on her in the break room; e) the custodian caught red-handed rifling through someone else's locker; f) the administrator who just might be on speed; and finally, g) the Employee Assistance counselor asking her, Melie, the one without the MSW, for advice. "I need you to tell me—what should I do?"

Melie took the long way back to the train station. Stopping to pick up the evening newspaper, she turned to page 13 to read her horoscope for the day: "Pisces, dear one, have you considered another line of work?"

Every year at this time, Melie vowed that by the next Christmas she would not again be sitting around the Reception area with her coworkers from the Benefits office, feigning undying loyalty to Merry Terry. Melie would never again hold up the "incredible" Christmas gift Merry Terry had just doled out to them. She wouldn't be forced to ooh and ahh.

If only . . . she said to herself. And, *why couldn't I leave?* Maybe no one would check that far back? The Big Old Secret, again, had kept her chained to her desk.

Last year they had each gotten a teensy weensy jar of jam—didn't Merry Terry's sisters run a farm? The year before was the travelling sewing kits, the ones hotels usually give you for free, with six strands of colored thread, a needle, a safety pin and, as a bonus, a needle threader. Merry Terry shouldn't have!

At this year's party the HR group put away their gifts (more jam), sipped their screwtop wine, and nibbled on party fare (stale potato chips and such). Merry Terry insisted they play charades and pretend to like each other though she constantly badmouthed each division to the other ("Employment, they don't do anything there—just blab blab blab to people").

Melie decided to shake things up a bit. She stood up, after downing three glasses of wine, and with Geena beside her to help carry the tune, she sang a little ditty she'd written to the tune of "Pop Goes the Weasel."

Pop Goes the Kidney?

The surgeon's in the operating room,
His secy's on the phone to Cuba,
The charts are a mess so he takes out a kidney
Instead of the fallopian tub-a!

She's been with him for 21 years
And shown up for almost five,
(He pays her out of petty cash)
And some of his patients are still alive!

This time tho' he's raving mad
That poor Mom's on dialysis
"Why did I give her commendables?
That night, it was only one kiss."

I just don't care—she's got to go,
I want her gone by tomorrow
Her sexy long legs and long blond hair
Have caused me too much sorrow.

When Melie looked up and saw Merry Terry slapping her thigh and even dour Lucille laughing, she decided they'd had enough fun and abruptly sat back down without finishing. Poor Geena was left standing, but with her usual aplomb, grabbed another glass of wine, tossed her golden mane over her shoulder, and led a toast: "To another wonderful year at Axis Mundi."

Terry mouthed, "Sit down."

Melie knew she'd hear about this from Merry Terry. She could add it to her repertoire of negativistic soul-crushing remarks at evaluation time in June. And maybe Melie'd slam the door on her this time and wish her dead, as she had wanted to do every year for the last ten.

Something somehow somewhere needed to change before next Christmas.

Saturday morning, having received no response to her postcard to the man upstate, Melie forced herself to go trekking with the Mountain Clubbers of New York City. They were heading for a ridge that would afford them a view of the valley below in all its snow-covered glory.

Twice she had stopped and taken off her left hiking boot to plaster her heel with gauzy stuff another hiker insisted she use. She hoped to come home with more than a corn, something she'd earned, like a boyfriend. This guy wasn't really her type. She intended to look around more during lunch break.

That was her secret agenda. Sometimes she did meet men this way; once in a while they turned into one-night stands. Not a naïve person, Melie nevertheless always thought they would be back. And one guy did come back—for his hat! (She'd kept his underwear.)

For company, aside from the "nut and berry crowd" she met here, she could depend only on Furryface, her ten-year-old cat, and the seven-year-old kid upstairs, whom she sometimes took to the movies. She passed her time on the weekends walking in the rain around the high school track, rewatching the video of *The Little Mermaid*, gobbling up any horror stories or twisted murder mysteries she found at the library, especially if you couldn't tell what was going to happen at the end.

The most important man in Melie's life thus far and maybe forever had been Leonard. The litigator. Four years before. Not once had she been suspicious of weekends when he had had to entertain out-of-town clients. Many times he had not been able to call her even for five minutes after he showered or before he went down to dinner with his "guests." Finally he was just not able to call her at all.

She'd left him three or four messages on his answering machine at two-thirty AM, but she could not find him. So painful and maddening to believe he could just disappear without saying anything! Not until then had she realized that she knew few of his friends and had never been invited to meet his family.

Here she was now talking to this hiker, a tall blotchy guy who claimed to know Leonard. This guy said that Leonard had married a girl of twenty-seven, a fitness trainer, who had relocated to New York City from Hong Kong several years ago.

"I see," she said in her professional voice which was pitched higher than usual. "How could I compete with that?"

"Pardon? Were you his girlfr—Did you know him long?"

Rapidly calculating, Melie figured that Leonard had continued to come by weekly to bang her, Melie, after meeting this Asian beauty. The bastard!

She listened as the guy went on to explain what a wedding it had been, how happy Leonard looked. Melie thought how rarely she had seen Leonard smile. He frowned a lot— when he tasted her cooking, looked around her basement apartment, or glanced at her thighs as she ran down to the edge of the water at the shore.

The view from the ridge was worth it. The peanut butter on rye, stale granola bar, shared raisins, and conversation with Leonard's colleague were not. Melie was itching to get home, into a hot bath, and then sit on the rug in her tattered green plaid robe as the Little Mermaid drifted along in a rowboat beside her prince, waiting to be released from soundless misery by a single simple soul-catching kiss.

CHAPTER V

SEX AND DEATH

The weeks and months rolled on. Nothing changed. Until . . .an afternoon in mid-March, when Melie, unbidden, stood at the entrance to Ye Olde Antique Shoppe and let herself be sucked once more into its vortex. *Nature abhors a vacuum,* Melie thought, *so maybe I am needed here. Expected.*

She stood suspended in an anteroom of sorts, cloudy and dim, light filtering in from distant windows. Sheaths of dust motes, whole galaxial milky ways, crisscrossed around her, gently entrapping her in their celestial design.

As she gazed upon the play of light against the surfaces, she strayed from her spot. Her right foot caught in a spoke of a wheel and she nearly toppled down into a tattered blue baby carriage. But she managed to right herself and brought forth from the ancient carriage, rocking slightly on its giant wooden wheels, a miniature white lace pillow, too big for a doll, too small for her own head. Impulsively she clutched it to her bosom like a packet of love letters and sighed, "Ohh."

"Well, *hello!*"

It was Him. Melie gasped, twitched, staggered backwards. *I should just get it over with and swoon,* she told herself. Sweaty and red-faced, she turned to face Ted Baer. "Where's...what happened to your beard?"

"Oh, that. . .you must be a tourist." He chuckled to himself. "I only put it on for tourist ladies."

Melie must have looked as if she were trying to catch flies. She had thought nothing could surprise her any more.

"It's an image thing, you see." Ted paused and moved closer. "I do remember you now. You came here in, what? About three months ago? Bought that green perfume bottle?"

"December." She cleared her throat. "When I came up to ski at Finn Mountain."

"Lady, you won't be skiing today. It's going on seventy degrees." He stared at her, challenging her to defend herself.

Melie blushed. "I thought I'd make another pass."

"Go ahead, lady." He grabbed a grayish remnant of undershirt off the top of a bookshelf and set about dusting some books. Her trained eye saw the sidelong glances he sneaked every few minutes.

She got busy examining his collection of wooden chests, trunks, cigar boxes, doodads. He busily liberated more dust motes, which were sent aloft to join their brother and sisters.

Suddenly a cry issued from the interior of the Shoppe. "Teddy-Baby! I need you!" squawked the little red and green woman of the house. "Now!"

Ted colored this time—but was it with pride? Did he really think that dumb parrot was his friend? "Excuse me, lady. Gotta feed Gladys. She's got some lungs on her, eh? I named her for my ex-mother-in-law." He turned and retreated into the depths of his Shoppe.

It is his cave, she thought. *And what the hell am I doing here?*

She knew the answer to that question, of course. She had to find a life. Quick. The noose was tightening. She was on her way to becoming interchangeable with the pitiful types she counseled every day. Here was someone like her, detached from human contact, available.

A little while later, Ted reappeared. By this time Melie was sitting in a child-size rocking chair, her knees almost touching her chin, arms wrapped around the pillow.

He gave her the once-over. She didn't care if he did.

"Miss," he began, "I'm brewing some coffee for myself. And Gladys…"

She looked up and caught his eyes. Gladys was perched on his left shoulder, pecking at his faux beard with her beak, pointedly ignoring the presence of their visitor. "No wonder it's red in the middle," she blurted out loud.

Ted grinned. "You see, Gladys has her ways. Like all women. That's why I can't wear it all the time, you see."

Melie nodded somberly. "I see."

"C'mon to the back, lady."

"I do need a pick-me-up," she said, wondering what he had in mind.

He extended a hand to help her out of the kiddie chair. "Sure you do. I'll fix you right up."

Gladys was not a happy camper. She strutted back and forth on the dirty perch outside her cage where Ted had placed her, advancing and retreating like General Patton. From time to time she paused to fix Melie with a beady black eyeball while gnawing on the splintered wood of her perch.

Not blind to the action, Melie sat on a stool behind the counter, sipping the coffee, strong with a touch of cinnamon. Ted was popping up and down from his stool to give another tweak to the layout of estate jewelry in a nearby display case.

"You like the coffee? I pick it up in the city every time I go down. One habit I never lost. And if I'm really splurging, I get some black Russian bagels from First Avenue."

Melie smiled politely and continued to keep one of her two good eyes on Gladys who seemed to make more noise whenever Ted spoke to his guest.

"So you make the trip all the way into the city?"

"Sometimes. By the way, Mel," he interrupted himself, "do you want to put that little suitcase away now?"

She glanced down at the overnight bag at her feet. "Oh, that." *What the hell should I do now? There must be a motel nearby. Or I could check that B&B.* She'd have to leave soon. "It's just fine where it is." She hoped she sounded stern.

Ted shrugged. They made some more small talk, and she tried not to stare at the big man's hands as he gestured or gape when a smile lit up his face. She realized she didn't have any sense in here of the outside world—the time, the weather, the century. She realized how comforted she felt, ensconced in a corner of the universe with Ted.

Ted stood up, stretching elaborately, like a bear reaching for honey. "Excuse me one minute. I gotta lock up."

She stayed in the position he had left her in until he came back, in part fearing a craniofacial attack by Gladys, first parrot-woman gladiator, in part stuck like a mote in a galaxy not her own.

"I'm going in the back room now for my four PM-er. Amazing how a good nap revives one. I can actually stay up to ten PM this way."

She noticed that he wasn't wearing his beard, and he wasn't smiling.

"Could you put Gladys in her cage?"

"Sure."

Melie watched as he gently stroked the head of his parrot and sweet-talked her back into her cage. Then he cast a last look at Melie and strode off into dimly-lit regions of the store.

He's daring me to follow him.

She glanced around the Shoppe for a sign or signal, some encouragement, and lo and behold, she found it: tacked to the calendar on the back wall, next to her business card, was the postcard she'd sent him months ago.

Many minutes later, she entered the back room. Ted was lying on the right side of a cream-colored ruffled and canopied double bed. He was facing the wall.

Melie stepped out of her shoes and crawled in beside him. Her dress was getting crumpled. She lay on her back, trying not to hold her breath. *I'm not going to think about this too much*, she promised. She decided to touch the small of his back, but when she turned toward him, he was staring straight at her.

"Why don't you make yourself right at home, lady?" he asked, grinning. His teeth were white, pointy, feral.

She reached out to him and ran her fingers through the downy fur, soft like a cat, on his upper left arm. She kept her eyes focused on his arm and shoulder. When his hand, then his tongue found her breast, then her nipple, she could only say, "Ohhh."

"Let's try that again," said Ted Baer, when he woke up from his nap. She'd been gazing out the window at the fading light while he slept, the sky orangey-pink, the sun touching down on the horizon just left of the mountain. She let herself be drawn into another embrace, grateful to be entrapped in this particular celestial design.

46

He does have kind eyes, she decided.

After drowsing for a while, Melie and her lover agreed it was time to get moving. She felt her whole body humming a tune she hadn't heard for ages. *I guess I made the right decision.*

"So, lady, where do we go from here? Ted asked, as he pulled on his jeans and a big orange tee shirt emblazoned with the logo of the local ale brewery.

Gee, he has nice shoulders. And such strong thighs. She'd always been partial to strong meaty thighs on men. Let others go for butts; she was a thigh girl. She giggled like a madwoman.

"Lady?"

He extended his hand and helped pull her from the soft nest of pillows and comforter.

"What time do you close up?"

"Anytime I want. Is there somewhere you need to go?"

Instead of being embarrassed by her own brazen behavior, Melie just went with it. "I was wondering if we could see your place?"

"The Manse?" He shook his head affirmatively. "Sure I'll take you over there."

She threw her clothes back on hurriedly. Once dressed, she commandeered a mirror and a brush, hoping to restore a little decency to her person by tamping down her wild curls, sprung like the springs on her old rollaway. No matter how much mousse or gel she glommed on, they gleefully defied her. The silly grin reflected there shocked her to her core. *Why, I look almost happy.* Melie picked up her suitcase. "All ready."

"Yes, you are," Ted said.

'Huh?"

"I mean, you seem to be a woman who knows her own mind."

He should only know . . .

He escorted her out of the Shoppe, grabbed Gladys and her cage, and locked up in what seemed like one fluid movement.

The Manse turned out to be a lakeside log cabin a few miles from town and the Shoppe. The front porch faced Finn Lake and the back deck opened onto the woods. A small shed with wood stacked against its side sat at the edge of the property. Stepping inside the cabin, Melie saw that there was just one open room with a sleeping alcove to the right, a big pot belly stove smack in the middle, a comfortable, broken-in settee facing the heat, and a table and two chairs by the back door. To the left was a small compact kitchen, and the bathroom was tucked into the back left corner.

"Manse, haha. I get it," she said to cover her embarrassment as Ted deposited her overnight bag and Gladys in the sleeping alcove. "Hard to get lost in here."

"Suits me. And Gladys."

Melie realized her New York sarcasm might be out of place up there in the sticks. "It looks . . .very comfortable. And airy. And the lake is superb."

"As I said, suits me. And Gladys."

In such a confined space, there was no escaping. Melie and Ted moved around a bit stiffly at first. He rummaged in the fridge and finally pulled out some hamburger meat; she stood by the back door and watched the stars come out. "Ted, come quick. A deer!"

"Yup."

"I think there's something wrong with his foot."

"He's lame, that one." Ted did not take his eyes off the hamburgers frying in the pan. "I leave apples in the back for him."

"Oh. Poor thing." Melie watched until the deer limped back into the woods, then she joined Ted in the kitchen alcove. She stood beside him, watching the burgers sizzle and pop. "Can I do something?"

He raised his eyebrows and licked his lips. "Absolutely." He put his arm around her shoulders and squeezed. "But first we need to get some vittles in us."

They sat at the little table with their hamburgers and some tomato and lettuce leaves and two glasses of a surprisingly good local craft beer, and tried to get to know each other.

"Ted, I noticed you had a stack of Jamie LaCourt mysteries in the Shoppe."

Ted looked up from his salad. "I'm a big fan of hers. Those characters—they're so grotesque. I mean, who acts like that? Where does she get them from?"

'I've read a lot of her stuff too. You never know how her stories are going to end, do you?"

"I can't figure her people out. Can you?"

"Well, no, but I'm probably not as shocked by what they do."

"How come, lady?"

"Just the nature of my job. I see a lot of eccentric behavior."

"I bet you do. Remember I'm a former New Yorker from the Bronx. I know the score. Listen, can I get you something else?"

"I'm good." Melie realized she felt as good as she sounded. She stood up and started gathering the plates.

"I can handle those," said Ted. "but can you find some music you like? Look on the bookshelves against the back wall."

Melie was still looking when she heard him creep up behind her. She turned her around in time for him to plant a big wet kiss on her lips. "Umm," she crooned.

"So you're enjoying my kisses, are you?" Ted beamed. "Haven't found anything yet?" He pulled out a record. "Leonard Cohen, know him? Great Canadian singer/songwriter." Ted put the record on the stereo turntable to play.

After the song finished playing, Melie said, "Can we hear that again? That's incredible. The lyrics, the music. And it's funny as hell."

"I tell you what, lady. Let's put it on and listen to it over there." Ted pointed to the large water bed that took up the entire sleeping alcove.

And so they went to bed.

But while Melie was upstate romping with Ted, her boss was at Axis Mundi romping with Death! Returning from her weekend at Finn Lake, Melie was stunned to learn that Merry Terry was D-E-A-D. She'd been struck down at her desk Friday at approximately six PM, done in by a heavy steel-grey filing cabinet that somehow loosened from its moorings and fell onto her small square grey body. She must have been pinned to the floor when twenty or so black looseleafs, filled with turnover statistics, job requisitions, and wage and salary tables, slid from the shelf above the cabinet, pounding her small square grey head into the thin grey industrial carpet. She never stood a chance.

Doug Milty, chief financial officer, was the one who had discovered her battered square grey body. Showing up at her office for a seven o'clock meeting on the advisability of installing a new HRIS system, word was he accidentally stepped on her bloodied hand, shrieked, and then fainted dead away. A cleaning lady heard the commotion, bravely investigated, and called the paramedics to come and take both bodies to the hospital. Doug woke up in the ambulance and ordered them to take him home.

Melie grasped the situation in a second. Foul play, and everybody had a motive!

Axis Mundi Medical Center was in total uproar, and HR was fast coming unglued without Merry Terry to rush people into corners and scare them into doing some work. The word around the Benefits office was that a twenty-five-year vet, Lucille, the records manager, a tall thin scowl of a woman, had been named acting HR director. Lucille was sitting in her office, working out her feelings, alternately sobbing into her messages, grinning wildly out the window, and punching her bulletin board with both fists.

Disoriented, Melie sought refuge behind her own desk and let her little staff gather round for comfort. Geena, Arielle, and Sukie filled her in on the little they knew, often talking at once. The police had kept them in the office until ten PM on Friday, "even though it was date night!" Geena advised. She was quite indignant over missing a prearranged b.d.o. (blind date opportunity).

"Oh, he was probably just a 'zero' anyway," she said to console herself. (Zero was HR parlance for a candidate not worth a second look, someone they hoped would not darken their doorstep a second time.)

Sukie and Melie exchanged a look. Melie allowed herself the luxury of rolling her eyes. Arielle laughed, but did she get the joke? She was only a kid. Sukie started in, mapping out the future of HR, while lamenting the loss of someone who had been taking small but visible steps toward enlightenment.

"How long would she have had to live to be human?" Melie asked. "You've said yourself everyone wanted to kill her. Just for starters, let's review: the time she advised Neurology to remove their water fountain because the registrars and administrative secretaries were drinking too much, putting the department over budget; the time she ordered that lovely, older, slightly befuddled billing clerk home to look for two hundred dollars in missing copayments and "grandma" slit her wrists; or the time she insisted surgery fire that homosexual receptionist because people weren't used to seeing "that" at the front desk of a world-class medical center." Melie rested her case.

Geena and Arielle were wide eyed but Sukie brushed her off. Sukie insisted that if they looked beyond this tragedy and the loss implied for the Quincents, they would see the chance, at last, to gain recognition (and even dollars?) from their steady hard work. She saw no impediment to Melie's becoming HR director in a few months' time.

(God forbid.)

The phones were ringing off the hook in the outer office, all 2,507 employees calling in to gossip, offer condolences (not necessary), clues, share conspiracy theories, and, of course, weep and wail and wonder if they were next. Everyone had come to the same conclusion: this was no accident. Why, they said, remember, that girl in Neurology had the same thing happen to her—a tipped-over cabinet— and she was still around to tell the tale. No, there was a murderer on the loose at Axis Mundi!

Merry Terry had been in her office from 5 PM on with the door closed. Was anyone with her? There was another door into her office through which a murderer could have slipped, unseen.

In the middle of morbid musings, Geena suddenly asked, "So what was it like? Finn Lake? You never told us why you were going back there."

Melie shooed her staff away. They knew little. She wasn't ready to talk about her adventures just then. She closed her fluorescents and sat in the dingy light filtering in from the avenue.

Merry Terry's whole life had been Axis Mundi Medical Center—fitting she should die there. It could have been me, Melie thought and silently nodded. She rested her head on her folded arms. She wondered what to think. Either she should have taken a day off long ago or she shouldn't have done so now. Had she made a mistake? Merry Terry had died with her boots on, literally. She wanted to feel sorrier for her, but all the times Merry Terry could have been human, all the times Melie saw a chance for her to be more humane . . .

Melie remembered a lunch they had had together on the occasion of Melie's birthday one year. Melie had ordered wine before her boss could veto it. Slightly tipsy, the two of them had discussed movies, books, vacations. Merry Terry had almost been like a normal person for an hour or two. That's when Melie realized: Merry Terry *chooses* to be hateful.

Melie lifted her head. *Damn if I'm going to wind up like Merry Terry.*

Lunchtime, Melie rounded up her staff and took them to the nicest French restaurant in the neighborhood. They were in a strange celebratory mood.

Who was covering the desk?

"What if there's an emergency?" Geena asked and then laughed at her own joke.

Today nobody much cared and everyone had an excellent appetite. They asked Melie if they really had to go back to the office for the afternoon. Melie told them they were going a bit far.

> Melie slumps in a booth in a diner on the Upper East Side, knitting. Merry Terry slides in beside her, resting her head with its grey helmet-like shape on Melie's shoulder. All Melie's efforts go into not shrinking away from her dead boss's touch.
>
> After an eternity, Merry Terry lifts her head and roughly turns Melie to face her. They are much too close for too many minutes. Melie has abundant time to take in the colorless dishwater face, the lack of any makeup to enliven the ordinary features, the boxy grey shirtwaist, the man's watch. Ducking beneath the booth, she doublechecks that Merry Terry is wearing her usual old lady black oxfords.
>
> Check.
>
> But she'll never be an old lady, Melie realizes.
>
> "Well?" Merry Terry says.
>
> Melie blurts out, "I knew you when you were dead."
>
> Merry Terry turns a fiery hue; she belches out smoke; she thrusts out a clawed hand to lay on Melie's heart to stop it.

Melie jackknifed in her bed, pulling frantically at the flannel night-shirt stuck to her chest. "You're dead. You're dead. You're dead," she insisted until she realized she was back in her own bedroom.

I didn't do it, she thought, and then wondered what she meant.

CHAPTER VI
CITY GAL GOES COUNTRY

The next day Melie worried that she herself had a far-from-iron-clad alibi. She could claim she had been with Ted, of course, canoodling. That scenario was one, however, she was not anxious to share with the pale-faced, pimply, pubescent detectives swarming around. She feared she might be one of their top suspects. Her shouting match with Merry Terry had been overheard by the entire Benefits office. Yet she overheard the detectives mumbling something about her being too short (?). No way could she produce a train ticket receipt for her trip to Finn Lake on Friday. At first she stuck stubbornly to her story that she'd left work Friday at noon and gone straight to bed with a migraine. No witnesses. And no history of migraines.

Don't they realize the murderer could have emptied the lower file drawers and rigged the cabinet to fall hours or even days ahead of time?

The poor boys aimed to be thorough. Where was she all weekend? No one—not the police, not her staff— had been able to reach her by phone. Backed into a corner, Melie reluctantly admitted she'd gone upstate to ski. Why had she lied? *I'm a private person and don't like others knowing my business.* She concocted a story with no role for Ted: she'd stayed alone at a B&B, relaxing, reading, strolling through the small town, shopping. Damn if they didn't check. Strangely, the Finn Lake Bed and Breakfast innkeepers corroborated that a Ms. Melanie Kohl had been having dinner in their rustic dining room at the time of the murder, and the next morning at six AM she'd taken full advantage of the Lumberman's Special (pancakes, bacon, sausage, ham, grits, eggs, blueberry, cranberry, and orange muffins). Melie had no clue where the innkeepers had gotten this mistaken notion or whom they were mixing her up with. They must have been thinking of her first visit there in December.

Others did not get off so easily. Even Arielle had been cross-examined two or three times and come out looking like a string mop the housekeepers had wrung out a time too many.

There was a small memorial service on campus at three PM. Melie said a few words; Sukie, a lot more—she had a religious nature and loved the spotlight—and Lucille cried and wailed and was almost keening. She acted like an official mourner from a small Mediterranean village. She made quite a spectacle of herself.

Merry Terry's family looked shell-shocked and nothing like her. They were stout, it's true, and on the short side, but seemed a lot more anodyne than their oldest sister whom whom they said they never quite understood.

Merry Terry's hubby, small, stooped, and thin almost to the point of disappearance, stared straight ahead at all times, even when facing a blank wall. *What bar girl would go home with the two of them?* Melie shuddered.

Finally, the Dean of the medical center thanked them all for their words of remembrance. He strode away from the podium, then scurried back to announce henceforth human resources would report directly to Douglas Milty, head of finance.

What? Merry Terry had always reported to the Dean of Axis Mundi Medical Center. This means Lucille will report to Milty who will report to the Dean. Melie didn't dare look at Sukie, Geena, or Arielle. She and Sukie walked back to their offices, trying to absorb the news. The two younger women lagged behind.

Kicking all pretenders to the HR throne aside, portly Doug Milty, CFO, had somehow made himself king.

"For a man who looks like his picture should be hung in the post office," Melie observed on the walk back, "he seems to be doing all right here."

He was the kind of man who made Melie uneasy, big and bald, eyes constantly shifting beneath bushy eyebrows, never looking directly at anyone, skin, the tint of plaster of Paris. He probably smelled—she had never gotten close enough to know—and his pants had that right-out of-the-dryer-in-the-basement look. About fifty, it was rumored he had been canned by Price Waterhouse before Axis Mundi's Dean gave him a leg up.

The first time Melie had had to sit with him in her office, the day he was hired, her radar was buzzing: *Enemy Aircraft*. His hands kept slipping below his belt to "adjust" himself.

"He's either a pervert or a self-mutilator. I can't decide which," she confided now to Sukie.

"Melie, I'm shocked. I know you're not as callous as you seem. He's a man with a few problems possibly . . ."

"Get off it, Suke," Geena interspersed, as she and Arielle ran to catch up with them. "He's 'off' with a capital 'O' and you know it."

Melie raised her eyebrows. Sukie succumbed to an attack of the giggles, holding her embroidered handkerchief up to her mouth, tears leaking from her eyes. Melie confined herself to a smirk. Poor Arielle strained to keep up with the developments.

Doug Milty was their new boss. "And we thought things couldn't get much worse," said Melie, pulling her staff into an impromptu brain-storming session in her office. "Let's see. What do we actually know about Uncle Milty?"

"Well," Sukie began, "nobody seems to like him much except the Dean, who I guess thinks he's doing satisfactory work."

Arielle said, "You can't get anyone in accounting or payroll on the phone when you have a question. If you do, they scream, 'Hold dawn—I'm busy' and hang up on you."

"Also," Melie added thoughtfully, "no new accounting or payroll pro-cedures have been implemented since he arrived three years ago. And no one knows what the old procedures were."

Sukie added, "His assistant, Annabelle, came to see me twice, very upset. He treats her like a file clerk."

"Yeah," said Arielle. "At lunch the other day, the clerks from account-ing were saying Doug never says hello when he comes in at ten-thirty."

Melie shrugged. "We're used to that anyway. Conclusions, gang?"

"We're cooked!" Geena said. Sukie, Melie, and Arielle bobbed their heads in agreement.

The next Tuesday Melie was summoned to Doug Milty's office in D Building.

"Melie, I'm putting you in charge of HR, reporting directly to me."

Melie strained to meet Milty's eyes, blinded by the sun coming in his window. "But Lucille—?"

"Lucille's gotta go out on disability. All she does is whack that bulletin board of hers. Tacks are everywhere. You can't step in there."

"I guess she's taking Terry's death a bit hard."

"Funny way to go, huh? Ho! Ho! At any rate, you'll have to tell Lucille she's finished." He cleared his throat. He puffed himself up. He popped a button. She winced.

"Are you leering at me, Doug?"

He gave her a menacing cross-eyed stare and let a punishing silence reign.

"What I mean is, Doug, Lucille's in charge of disability leaves at Axis Mundi. She knows how that works. A doctor would have to certify that she needs the leave. We can't—"

"Come in to see me in the AM and tell me how it went. I don't want to see her around anymore, understand?"

"Also she and I don't have the greatest rapport . . ."

He came around his desk and put his plump hand on her shoulder. And squeezed. Hard.

Melie rushed back to HR and went straight to Sukie's office, where she stood in the doorway. "By the way, Sukie, Uncle Milty's coming on to me!" Melie strove to say this in her most offhand manner.

"Why, that's outrageous!" Sukie got up and pushed past Melie, making a beeline for Melie's office. "We have a policy against that, you know." Sukie started wildly rummaging through Melie's HR Worlds, legal bulletins, and such, looking for Axis Mundi Medical Center's "Just Say No to Sex Harassment," a two-color brochure of which they were all so proud.

"Stop it. Suke!"

Sukie stopped midstream and gaped at Melie.

"Suke, I'm serious. Don't you think I know our policy? Who do you think wrote it? Who's handled all the sexual harassment cases around here? Merry Terry?"

"No, I know you have, Melie. Don't yell at me. I'm just trying to help." She sat opposite Melie then and wrung her hands in silence for a few minutes.

"Oh. God," she concluded.

Melie stumbled through the rest of the week. Luckily Doug was at an out-of-state Accounting Conference and seemed to have forgotten about HR for the moment. Given his conduct, how in the world was she ever going to discuss Keisha Anne Woods with him? Where was Merry Terry when she needed her?

On Friday Melie walked into the Ye Olde Antique Shoppe unannounced, letting the dust mote galaxies envelop her, spiral down her body from her bouncing brown curls to her HushPuppy-clad toes. She moved purposefully through the thick speckled atmosphere toward the counter in the back where Ted was sure to be.

Ted frowned a little when he saw her, turned away to mark a date on the calendar, and muttered, "Back, are you?"

Melie circled behind the counter, reached up and kissed him on both cheeks. She held on to him a moment, poised on her tippy toes, resting her cheek against his. "I missed you."

Ted seemed to shrug (or shiver?). He looked around his Shoppe, over at Gladys, then down at Melie's soft head of black-brown curls. He shrugged or shivered again; then he grabbed Melie close and rested his head on hers.

"You tourists!'

Is it possible? Am I finally to have my own person, a boyfriend? It's not too late?

She had not had too many lucky breaks in life: she had been born to two parents raised during the Depression, each encased in their own protective shell, with limited outreach to the wider world. After Mom squeezed out one child, she felt she had made quite enough sacrifices for the common good. Her time could now be devoted to her real object of desire, herself. Dad, alternately ignored or humored during his growing-up years in semi-poverty, had learned to ask little of life and other people, seeking his pleasures in solitary pastimes (reading, going to movies alone, following sports and politics). Mom needed Melie and anyone else in the immediate neighborhood to fawn over her and exclaim, "My, you really are amazing!" Dad just needed to be left alone—do not make too much noise ("Get that baby out of here!"), let him read the paper; do not divert his wife's attention away from him; and certainly, do not ask him for anything.

So Melie was damaged goods from the start. She got herself to college, tuition free in those days. Dad felt she was wasting her time: "Those are four years you could be earning a living as a secretary." Mom, not to be outdone, started taking college classes at night. Following a health crisis in her senior year, Melie dusted herself off, left school, and got a job as a secretary in a manufacturing plant where she soon moved up to office manager and then personnel director. She taught herself what she needed to know. After eight years at the plant, she was laid off and her job passed on to her secretary. Six weeks of answering ads landed her the position at Axis Mundi Medical Center. Suddenly she was in the Big Time.

Love life? Melie tended to run from connections, more comfortable being on the outside looking in. But here was a chance. She couldn't drop the lifeline that had been extended to her —or that she had grabbed onto.

Melie vowed never to turn Ted down (for sex), to be soft and yielding, to be a true partner in crime. She would help him with his business, smooth relations with the customers, organize his paperwork. Did he need her to do this? She would not stop to ask. She absolutely would not play games with him and would overlook any he played with her. The courtship would progress like this: Melie would chase Ted down to his hidey holes and burrow right in after him, blocking up the entrance. There would be no escape.

But humans can't stop themselves from playing games, can they?

The timing was so perfect for this relationship, Melie so ready, Ted seemingly so amenable. What should have been awkward wasn't; their differences were less a rockblock than a bridge they took turns running across. She attributed their ease with each other to their unique, mature, superior personalities. Her immigrant grandparents, she knew, would simply have said the coming together of Ted and Melie was *"beshert"* (preordained). *So be it.*

After their first encounter in the back room, she had asked, "Would you like it if I came back sometime?" Ted had acted surprised, in a good way she thought, then responded, "Suit yourself, lady." She'd been unsure what to make of that response until he put his hands on her waist, lifted her up, and swung her around the room. "Whee," she screamed.

Melie trained Ted to expect her almost every weekend. "Can you meet the 8:15 PM train next Friday?" she'd ask when he dropped her off on Sunday. And there Ted would be, motor running on his rust-colored pickup truck, a big smile stretched across his face. He'd jump out of the truck, greet her with two big smackeroos, one on each cheek, grab her overnight bag and toss it in the back. Then he'd hold the door open so she could enter like a lady. They'd race to the cabin and the weekend would begin, usually with a bang.

They quickly developed routines in their time together. She learned to wait on customers and chat them up, but she arranged to make herself scarce if they had any kind of complaint. She puttered around his small vegetable garden, hiked around the lake, went out rowboating with him. She loved the breeze in the night air, the forceful way he tumbled her about, the tempo of the days spent doing nothing much. She laughed with him when he poked gentle fun at the briskness of his little businesswoman and the serious, staccato way she had of speaking. She could just about keep it together at Axis Mundi weekdays, knowing that the weekend was a few short days away. She hoped the boy detectives would continue to ignore her and worried that they might not.

Things were going swimmingly as fickle April with her sudden downpours gave way to the temperate months of May and June and finally the summer was full upon them.

Over breakfast mid-July, eyeing Gladys, Melie asked the obvious question. "Why does your animal hate me, Ted?"

"Wait till you meet my children!"

"Hmm."

"So Melie, tell me something about your work," said Ted, deftly changing the subject.

"Other than my boss being found murdered?" *I guess I should mention it?*

"What was that?" Ted's wrinkled brow was just inches away. She reached over and smoothed it. "You'll have to wait for the sitcom to come out."

"No, really."

"You first. And last. Once is enough for me—I don't have the "*koyekh*" to relive it."

"The who?"

"It's Yiddish—it means God-given strength. Or at least that's what I think it means."

"I get it. Like moxie?"

"Close enough but that's *chutzpah*. Anyway, your week?"

"I bought eggs from my neighbor, Helen, these eggs in fact. Cause I knew my city gal needed to know what a real egg tasted like."

"Yeah, right. I don't eat when I'm not with you."

"You do, City Gal. Cardboard and pressboard and sawdust and spit."

"Hmm . . . yummy!"

"A few more weekends with me and you'll pink up just fine."

"Blow up, more like it!"

After clearing the breakfast dishes and washing up together, Ted drew Melie over to the back door and stood behind her with his arms wrapped tightly around her. "Mel, spill the beans. What do you mean your boss was murdered?"

Melie sketched in the general picture for him in all its gory detail, but omitting the strange guilt she felt about how Merry Terry had met her end.

"Your staff was . . . happy she died? And this was four months ago?"

"Ted, not just my staff. You could say the reaction was wholesale glee. By everyone."

"What kind of people do you have at Axis Mundi?"

"All kinds, Ted. All kinds."

"What worries me is: do they suspect you, Melie?"

"Me? I'm the one who puts the pieces back together, not the one who blows them all sky high." *What a cool character! Bravo!*

"There's a murderer on the loose though and—"

"No one thinks it's going to happen again. Trust me. It won't."

"Just watch yourself, Mel." Ted turned her around and planted a big one on her kisser. "I don't want to lose you just yet."

"And why is that?"

Ted had a surprise. Late afternoon, he pulled Melie forward by the hand. Then put his two hands on her back, gently pushing her into the warehouse-turned-auction house. They sat near the front with rows of fold-up chairs filling the hall on all sides.

"Where's the exit, Ted?" Melie asked, a little breathless.

"Shh . . . Mel. It's about to begin. See, there's Jakey. Some say he used to be a high school social studies teacher."

"With no front teeth?"

"Huh? Oh, that's probably since he moved up here and went to seed like the rest of us."

Melie immediately poked her index finger into Ted's mouth.

"Am I all there, lady?"

She nodded. "Anyway, I think . . ."

"Shh."

For the next few hours, Jakey had his mostly toothless crew bring forth rusted ten-speeds, farm equipment, a double-doored like-new refrigerator, stamp collections, a World Book Encyclopedia 1964, Billie Holiday records, 45s, saucers without cups, cups without saucers, motorcycles, washtubs, and a handheld vibrator.

Ted couldn't resist a huge black wrought-iron bird cage for twenty dollars. "I'm gonna paint it fire-engine red," he announced. "Gladys'll like that." Melie purchased a large wooden salad bowl and presented it to Ted.

Later that night, when Melie had revived a little after a nap in the pickup truck, they headed home and went shopping for their dinner in the back garden. Then they "cooked a salad." Their hands met over the new salad bowl. There was something satisfying and earthy about it: Ted's bulky fingers, chucking in the arugula and walnuts, the perfect counterpoint to Melie's delicate movements as she sprinkled in sprouts and wheat germ. They munched First Avenue black Russian bagels, drank strong coffee, and talked into the wee hours about their lovelong day.

CHAPTER VII

SPILLING THE ONE BIG SECRET

"You make me laugh," Ted said as they were getting dressed one Saturday morning.

"Me? How?" asked Melie, as she poked around the alcove, trying to locate her socks. Something occurred to her and she stopped in her tracks. "Are you mocking me?"

"Your comments on people here for instance," Ted continued, unfazed.

Melie considered this new information and decided to accept it. Her staff thought she was funny. They, Lucille and even Merry Terry had laughed at her Christmas song. *Why not take advantage of this opening?* "What else do you like about me, Ted?"

After a few minutes pause, Ted went on. "I guess I'd have to say, your energy."

Taking a seat on the edge of the bed, Melie struck a pose. Jutting out her bosom, crossing her legs, tilting her head just so, she hoped like hell the message read "come hither" rather than "I'm stuck and I can't get up."

"Yes, that's part of it," admitted Ted, a big smile plastered across his face, as he sauntered over and pushed her down flat on the bed.

Never one to leave well enough alone, Melie stilled his roaming hands. With a small serious expression, she questioned, "But what about my karma?"

Ted sat back, straddling her body, and put on his goofiest expression for her.

"Your . . .caramel . . . .What?"

"Now you're making me laugh," she said. I love you, she wanted to add, but feared his reaction or lack of one. "Don't let me keep you from whatever you were doing."

Ted made good use of the leeway she had granted him, to their mutual delight.

A week or so later, lying abed one lazy morning after they'd been talking about themselves, Melie understood he was trying to figure her out, so confident one minute, so shaky and on edge the next.

"What is it you want to know, Ted?

Ted just gave her a look.

"Yes, you're right. I am jumpy and quick to panic."

"Over little things. The coffeemaker overflowing yesterday, Gladys making a little mess."

"Right. It is work-related. But don't even ask. I can't leave."

"Why not? With your background—"

"Why? I . . .can't tell you."

"Tell me."

Melie gazed deep into those eyes of his for a full minute—it wasn't like Ted to insist— then rolled to the other side of the bed. "Just don't look at me."

Ted obligingly ducked his head back under the covers.

"I've had this job for ten years. Survived Merry Terry. Literally."

"Who's that again?"

"Never mind. Do you know I've had every physical symptom of stress one can have? The only department I haven't visited is neurology and that's probably in my future! And I've barely scraped the surface in psychiatry."

Ted stuck his head out for air. "What kinds of symptoms?"

"Oh, let's see. High cholesterol, high blood pressure natch, mysterious eyelid swellings, idiopathic laryngitis, involuntary tics in my left eye, idiopathic colitis. . ."

"What is that?"

"Oh, just my middle name. And I'm only thirty-nine! I mean, forty."

"And I thought I was robbing the cradle!"

"You are. You are. Can you breathe in there?" Melie pulled down the comforter hiding his face. Ted pulled it back up.

"So tell me already. I'm on your side."

Aren't those the most beautiful words in the world? Solar flares burst forth inside her skull, dazzling her for a moment.

"I was in my last semester of college. On a cold snowy night, I hitched a ride to a party given by a friend in my Comp Lit class."

Hearing her pause, Ted grunted.

"His name was Bill. Can you believe he was 6'4?"

"Hmm. You must have looked like his child."

"I guess . . . . Well, I thought he was kinda handsome . . . ."

"What happened? Melie?"

Melie took a deep breath and let it all spill out.

"He always said he would take care of anything that might come up. And it did. Come up. The contents of my stomach one morning."

"Geez."

"Yep, I was pregnant. I went to Student Health, where they gave me a big shot of some hormone and then I had, like, six periods in the next month. I was even rushed to the ER, hemorrhaging, and they kept asking me what I had done to myself. As if—"

"So . . ."

"Ted, like an idiot, I just left school. I couldn't handle it anymore."

"What about the guy?" Ted poked his head out of the covers and half sat up.

"I don't know. I left and never saw him again. I heard he was dating other girls, not just me."

"Sure he was. Nothing unusual there. Then what?"

"So I never got my degree, Ted. I'm missing sixteen credits. I lied in my application to Axis Mundi, I've been lying for ten years, for which I could get fired at any point!"

"But they never checked?"

"That was ten years ago. Now HR sends everything out to a background checking firm."

"Got it. But I think you could risk it. With all your experience . . ."

"No, another company would find out. Everybody checks. I'll probably get fired at Axis Mundi one of these days. Just before she died, Merry

Terry ordered a review of all the background checks on medical center employees.

"Why?"

"All because she couldn't locate Gerald Gutierrez's file. Also the fact that he killed his lover. And know what? He'd gotten all "commendables" on his last performance appraisal!"

"I'm not following all that. Aren't you in the clear now? Merry Terry is dead."

"Maybe. The thing is I don't think I can do this work any longer!" Melie's voice quivered. "I can't go into it. I don't like to get queasy on my day off." She curled into a fetal position, her back to Ted.

"C'mon here then, lady. Show me your Melie-belly!" Ted pulled off the covers and started kissing her soft smooth tummy as she gave in to giggles in spite of herself.

Of course, what else would he do?

The trouble started a couple of weeks later at Sunday breakfast, which had been going peacefully. The weather was warm and sunny with the hint of hotter, humid air lurking just around the corner. She'd filled her belly with a stack of Ted's special applesauce pancakes, and all was right with the world until suddenly it wasn't.

The trouble was Gladys. *This is a war,* Melie realized. Gladys was doing her usual: squawking loudly every time Melie opened her mouth to talk to Ted. Once they looked over and she was sure to have their attention, she would strut into the limelight (in this case the wooden perch outside her cage) and proceed to clean her feathers in a most meticulous manner, wrapping her pointy beak around each one and salivating along the length of it.

"What are you looking at, Ted?" Melie asked.

"Why, did you ever see such colors in your life? She's so vibrant," he observed, gazing at Gladys lovingly. "My little redhead."

She knows I look my worst at breakfast. Melie lounged at the breakfast table, draped in Ted's old washed-out City College sweatshirt. *I am drab.* She got up to fetch her new orange and green polka dot scarf which she had left thrown over a chair in the sleeping alcove.

"Shredded!" she screamed.

"What's that?"

"She's gotta go, Ted," she announced, striving to control her voice. She waved the wrecked scarf in the air. "Exhibit A."

"Never. Don't even go there, Mel. She's been with me through thick and thin."

"I see. So am I to understand my happiness isn't important to you?"

Ted picked her up then and twirled her around the room till she was laughing and crying and pleading for him to stop. He deposited her back in her chair. "You'll get used to her. She has her ways. You have yours."

Gladys flew over to the table and landed on Ted's shoulder where she hopped up and down gleefully. Melie picked up her half-drunk coffee—was that a dirty bird seed at the bottom of the cup? Her gorge rose. She held the cup up for Ted to see, but he and Gladys were too engrossed in their love fest.

Melie got up to scrub out her cup, make a fresh pot of coffee and to fetch that magazine she'd seen lying around. Some nice butterfly nets in there just might come in handy, sooner rather than later.

"What're you thinking of doing today, lady?" Ted asked, coming over to his front window, Gladys on his shoulder. He surveyed his front lawn, the path leading down to the lake, the blue sky overhead, and seemed pleased with it all.

"Let me finish my coffee and then I'll look through the local paper here . . . what's it called again? Ted?"

"Ted?"

Ted puffed away on one of his sweet-smelling pipes, still gazing out the window, while letting Gladys get on with her bizarre grooming rituals.

Is Gladys trying to stick her beak up his nose and clean those feathers? Yuck! Melie jumped up. "Where I come from, Ted, I'm used to being answered when I talk."

Ted looked her way, grinning. "Where you come from? Ha! Who're you kidding? New Yorkers are just yelling at each other all the time or jabbering into empty space. Honking or hollering. They ain't talking to you, they can't even hear you! Why—"

Melie opened the front door and took a deep cleansing breath. Ted placed Gladys back in her cage, and stepped quickly behind Melie to immobilize her with his famous Baerhug. "There, there. Now I do believe it's called *FK*."

"FK? Oh, yes, that's what we call it too." She turned towards him, smiling, batting her eyes, her bad mood forgotten.

"*FindersKeepers*, silly! The newspaper for Finn County."

"Oh, right." She pushed the door closed and began clearing the table.

Ted shook his head, amused, refilled his cup, and then headed back in Gladys' direction.

"So anyway, I was thinking that there's probably a listing of events in *FK*, Ted. Maybe something interesting's going on."

"Maybe."

"We could go to a country fair or pick apples, something like that."

"How about fishing?"

"Again? I mean, we did that last weekend."

"Yeah?"

"Well, I'd like to try something different."

"Fishing's different."

Melie said nothing. She stood immobile in front of the sink filled with their dirty dishes.

"You didn't like it?"

"Sure, fishing's okay." She turned on the hot water and began washing the dishes. "I mean, you really seem to enjoy it. You know what you're doing."

"But I'm ready to teach you everything!"

"Yes, I appreciate that. But, just the same . . . ." Melie finished cleaning up. She walked over to the back window, scanned the backyard, searching for an alternative. *Where was that darned paper?*

"You don't like it? Ted continued. "But, lady, what I don't get is . . . what's not to like?"

"Why are you taking this so personally? You're making me uncomfortable. How about more coffee?" Melie went over to the kitchen counter and brought the coffeepot over to the small round table, smoothing out the mauve and green tablecloth before setting it down and sitting down herself.

Ted frowned as he put down his pipe on the little table ashtray near the settee. "I've had enough." He stood awkwardly in the middle of the room.

"Don't pout. You look like a three-year-old." *Was there a sudden chill in the cabin?* She sensed the need to make amends and be speedy about it. "It's honestly not my thing. Fishing. It's almost kinda . . ." She raised her cup to her lips and drank.

"Say it, dammit!" She looked up; Ted's eyes bored into hers.

"Boring!" she yelled. Her hand flew up to cover her mouth. She clutched her coffee cup tightly, keeping her eyes on the table. *Now I've done it!*

Ted fetched the bag of birdseed and sprinkled some inside Gladys' cage. Then he said to no one in particular, or perhaps only to Gladys: "I'll be back when the fish get tired of me—or bored!" He picked up his tackle box and rod and left the house. Melie watched out the window as he cut across the road towards the lake.

She began pacing the kitchen soon after, drinking more coffee, folding and refolding the paper. She grabbed a jacket off the hook and started out the door, then came back in and hung the jacket on the back of a chair. She washed the two cups and looked over at Gladys. "Gladie, I think you might have won that round!"

The bird nodded up and down.

Melie stood at the window, biting her lip. Gladys had climbed back out of her cage—*He left the door open!* Melie didn't dare put her back in. Gladys hadn't said a word since early morning, except a little witch's shriek at the climactic word, "boring," and she said nothing now. She was a bird who kept her own counsel.

Melie called a cab to take her to the train and returned to the city with more time than usual to take care of her laundry, cleaning, shopping, and other meaningless tasks and to wonder why she was so good at other people's problems.

That night Melie dreamed of The Twins:

Two Italian sisters, one with dark curly long hair (the "wild one"); one with straight short black hair (the "plain one"). Every night they have group sex with men. They wonder about how to refer to this activity—should they call it "mixing it up" or "fraternizing"?

Melie (the "plain one") sees the other one sit on a bench where five men are seated. Then she says to herself, "So that's how it goes. She sets it up and I just tag along."

They are in middle age now; the plain one has grey in her hair at the sides, maybe the wild one too. The plain one wakes up in the morning after a night of group sex and goes downstairs. She looks in a box and her sister is lying in there, dead! She is upset and cries.

Now she is out on the street. A young man (thirtyish) walks by pushing a baby in a stroller. He tells Melie that she shouldn't be upset. Melie thinks he is the lover/husband of her sister.

An Italian mother, short, gray, a trim woman, comes by and makes a sign with her forefinger near her head to indicate to the man that Melie's crazy.

A car (mafia?) comes along and stops, signifying danger? Melie picks up the baby and cries. They take the baby away. Melie loved her!

Back to Axis Mundi, dealing with jittery staff, all the incomplete projects that were waiting for Merry Terry to put her stamp on them, the grievances and employees in imminent danger of harassment . . . . *Who's going to help me now with Babs? Tamis? Merry Terry always handled the faculty. Lum, the embezzler? Do we fire her first, press charges, and then investigate her racial discrimination charges? Or vice versa?*

On this particular Monday, Melie felt herself shift from bad to worse. Her abdominal cavity swelled in a skywardly direction, like a blimp filled with nitrogen.

She sat on her hands to keep herself anchored to the swivel chair with the torn brown vinyl scar up its back.

She gulped mugs of tepid water brought in by Arielle from the rusted water fountain in Reception and squeezed her eyes shut to ward off evil thoughts.

Why am I here? was the silent scream.

Birds in the North Country fell to Earth along a quiet stretch of stream.

Why hasn't he called? What have I done?

The empty woods echoed.

CHAPTER VIII
DESPERATE MOVES

"Babs, your doctor put you on long-term disability leave for your 'anxiety.' We've granted you another six months of personal leave starting a few weeks ago. You don't need to come in to work. Or come here. I'll let you know when it's safe to come back. Babs?"

Melie turned away from the window and the air. Axis Mundi's air conditioning was on the blink and this early August weather was a bit heavy and humid for her taste. She opted for some recommended therapeutic eye contact with her client. But Babs gave no sign of having heard. She stayed as she was—upper body splayed across Melie's desk, pincushion butt rising out of the chair.

Melie saw that sometime in the last fifteen minutes, Babs had knocked over the mini cactus plant near the phone. Knobby bits of plant, some gravel, water and sand floated atop the papers on her desk. Would anything sprout?

Babs lifted her head and her heat-seeking reddened eyes located Melie and locked onto their target.

"Why did you walk out?"

"Walk out? Babs . . . what?"

"It's just that I don't understand. Why?"

"Walk out?"

Melie pulled nervously at her turtleneck. Her eyes darted around the office, seeking a diversion. Defeated, she looked back and met Babs's gaze head on. "I can't believe this. Who told you about me?"

Babs blinked and shook her head. "Aren't we friends, Melie? After all we've been through? We're here to help each other. I know you, Melie, of all people, believe that. So . . . why leave? Ted sounds like such a nice man."

Melie walked back to her seat across from Babs and sat down. *How can this be happening?*

She said not a word to Babs, instead focused on moving the papers around on her desk. After a few minutes Babs took the hint and left. When Melie opened her top desk drawer, she found her journal lying there. Open. *Dirty snooper!*

Before bed Melie thumbed through her little red Chinese brocaded address book. Every year for the last ten years, she had picked up a new one in the bookstore downtown. And every year without fail she had copied over all the names and addresses and telephone numbers (day and evening) of all the people she knew and thought she would still be knowing in the coming year. Problem was every year the book shrunk a little more. And she really needed someone to talk to.

She thumbed the pages slowly, careful not to dog ear them. She liked the creamy rich paper with the pale grey barely visible words. So delicate. So subtle. Name. Address. Tel. Code. No.

She especially liked the two fishermen (!) with their long poles standing in a gondola eternally floating under the aqua and yellow leaves of a nearby tree, gliding past two peasants (father and son?) working diligently and companionably in a field outside their bamboo hut.

Early each year she would inscribe names with great care, but by the end of the summer, many entries had been whited out and the creamy pages began to swell and bloat.

Tonight, though she searched forever, she knew she would not come upon one name. It was therefore true and confirmed. She only needed an official-looking stamp that said:

> **YOU HAVE NOT ONE FRIEND IN THE WORLD**

She was really alone. Alive but alone.

She shut the tiny book. "I should throw you away."

But she tucked it carefully into the top drawer of her night table, sighed, and shut the light.

A little later that week, Babs dropped in to ask if she could sit in Melie's chair. Melie threw the rest of her salad in the garbage and nodded. She could see no harm in it. Babs took her chair and Melie settled herself into the visitor's chair. The effect was startling.

"What I mean is . . . I don't hear a peep from him, Babs."

"Have you tried calling?"

"What?"

"Is everything all right?"

"How would I know? None of my "relationships" have gone much past casual dating."

"Melie, the Answer Woman. Sex?"

"That's fine."

Babs threw her a studied sidelong glance.

"Actually, it's lovely."

"Everything you say in this room is absolutely confidential . . ."

"Shut up, Babs." Melie paused to swallow a sip of tepid coffee vendor coffee before continuing. "I show up Fridays, call from the station, and he comes to get me in his pickup. When we get to the cabin, he messes around with Gladys while I shower. Then we hop into bed."

"No dinner?"

"That's after. We eat liverwurst, mustard, and cucumber sandwiches in our bathrobes out on the deck if it's a nice night, not raining or anything."

"Sounds yummy. Then?"

"We make love again and drift off to sleep."

"How does Saturday go? I can guess how it begins."

"Saturday night we dress up—boots, nice jeans, and shirt—and go to Lucian's, a steakhouse, then go next door where there's a different band each week."

"Dancing?"

"Not so much. Just a drink or two. We might hold hands."

"Aw. That sounds romantic. Then . . .let me guess. You go home and make love again and then again Sunday morning?"

"Actually, I'm not one for doing it in the AM."

"Learn, girl, learn!"

"Anyhow, do you want to hear the rest?"

Babs clammed up immediately and focused her wide blue-gray eyes on Melie. She sat back in Melie's chair, obedient.

"That's it. Sunday we spend puttering around the house and garden. Last time I helped Ted paint his tool shed, and we took a ride into town."

"So during the week he never calls and neither do you? Not even to confirm the time of arrival Friday night?"

"Once I called to say I'd be on a later train."

"And he said?"

"Okay. Just 'Okay.'"

"Don't you think of him when he's not around?"

Melie stared into a corner of the ceiling, and after a few seconds recounted the fishing story, their first fight, how they each went their separate ways. And how she'd stayed home two weekends in a row and not heard a peep out of him.

"Go back. Take a hike in the woods around the lake. See what he's really doing."

"Huh?"

"Melie, child—there are women out there who like to spend the day fishing."

Melie turned an alarmed face toward Babs. Her heart was doing flipflops in her chest. "You think—"

"Listen to me, Answer Lady, time to ask Teddy Bear some questions."

Melie turned her head away from Babs, striving to regain composure, and stared out her grimy window. From that angle, she could see nothing, absolutely nothing.

Melie knew she tended to reach out and then pull back abruptly, as if her fingers had been burned on the proverbial oven door. She knew also that outwardly she appeared to underreact, after years of nodding solemnly to punctuate the most godawful confessions, and of permitting herself only a small murmur of "I see, hmm." Inwardly though she was one hot reactor, the hottest, as bubbling hot as lava spewing from the peak in Pompeii.

Now she had to wonder, to ponder. What did Ted see? Or know? It was maddening to think he accepted her cool exterior; it was very scary to think otherwise.

Maybe he wasn't calling during the week because he hadn't yet realized that she cared for him. She longed to tell him, but what if . . .? There seemed many hurts possible, risks all over the place, danger even. She wasn't sure she could bear to learn of his indifference. She had just started blossoming, filling out, seeing colors for the first time. She felt herself shrivel up into black stringy vegetal matter just at the thought of his disappointing her.

Up till now she had refrained from calling him. But tonight yogurt and cornflakes were not enough company. For one thing, they were too cold and too colorless.

"Ted, it's me."

"Melie? Anything the matter?"

"No, not really. I just wanted to see how you were."

"Oh. Uh, let's see. Actually, I'm in a little rush right now, getting ready to play cards over at Sam and Helen Call's."

"Sorry. I won't keep you."

"Wait. Hell, I got time. Mel?"

"Yes?"

"So what are you doing?"

"Nothing much now."

"Job driving you crazy? Bad day?"

"Oh . . . no." *Why am I so tongue-tied?*

"I better get moving." He paused. "Will I . . . will I see you this weekend?"

"Could be."

"Good. Thanks for calling. Lady. Mel?"

"Bye."

"Yeah, bye."

"That went well!" Melie announced to Furryface, who did not deign to open her eyes. She scrunched down in her bed and pulled the covers up to her chin. She went to sleep with the lights on and a half-full bowl of cereal balanced precariously on her bedside table.

She woke up the next morning at the usual time, but when she

79

punched the alarm clock, it struck the table and fell smashed to bits on the floor. Without much thought, she picked up the bowl of soggy flakes and threw that down too.

In the bathroom she washed her face and hands, then glimpsed herself in the mirror. What a sinister grin! She liked the way it made her look—unpredictable, uncaring, dangerous.

In record time she dressed, called in sick, and consulted the necessary timetables.

"By Jove," she said aloud, "he's not going to get away with this!"

Melie was still grinning when she stepped off the train at Finn Lake on a grey Wednesday morning and went hunting for a taxi.

Arriving at the cabin she marched right in, expecting Ted to be at work. But instead she found him in full morning *deshabille*, lying on the settee in front of the TV, holey undershirt, unholy boxer shorts, and bare feet, scratching places where the sun don't shine.

"Ted!"

"Mel!" He jumped up and just gaped at her.

She went straight to the breakfast nook and plunked her bag down.

"Stop looking at me like that please."

He gathered himself together and poured two cups of First Avenue coffee. "You just gave me a bit of a fright, that's all. Can we sit . . .?"

They sat down stiffly on either end of the settee.

When she didn't start talking, he asked, "So, lady, what brings you to this neck of the woods on a Wednesday?"

She shrugged.

"I see. Very interesting. Have a hard roll then."

She did. "Why aren't you at work, Ted?"

He raised an eyebrow, seemed about to respond, then just shook his head. He grabbed another roll.

"Ted!"

"What?"

"Are you ready for that ball you told me about? Victoriana? The one you organize—"

"Ready? Mel, we got weeks yet, until the end of September. But can you believe it? A dozen girls came into the Shoppe, and me and Helen, who's somewhat of a seamstress, set them up just fine with antique silk and lace gowns, long satin gloves, pointy little shoes—we even found a few wide brimmed hats, like out of a movie! They looked so pretty. You're going to love this event—better than an evening at the Met!"

She studied her nails. Ragged. She'd never been to the Met. "What is going on?"

"How do you mean?"

"In our . . . relationship?" She almost choked.

"What do you want me to say?" He was sneaking glances at the TV.

"What do you think . . . of us?"

"Us?" He appeared to be having trouble translating what she was saying into his native language.

"Forget it!"

He got up and stood beside her, pulling her up to face him. "Look, love, I don't know what you'd like me to say. You show up here with no warning—I think maybe I'm being robbed—and you start demanding things. I have a slight hangover—"

"Answer me, damn you!"

"Lady," he said, dropping back onto the settee, "first off, I don't like my woman to be cussing that way, and second off, I don't 'do' relationships."

For the next ten minutes Ted stared at a TV show about making it on Wall Street. The show ended; he shut the TV off and went to shower. He came out in a funny antique nightshirt and a silly nightcap, pirouetted in front of her, then stretched out in the sleeping alcove. It was 11:35 AM.

"Lady, I'm having trouble with something in here. Can you help please?"

(She couldn't help herself.)

Later—

"To what do I owe. . .?"

"Oh, shut up, Ted."

"Now she wants me to keep quiet?" He began to shake her.

"It's just that I know what you're going to say."

He let go of her. "How can you?"

"It's just that what you say, Ted, is so . . . limited!"

"Now she's telling me I'm stupid. Get outta my bed!" He started shoving her until she hung over the bed screaming for mercy. Then he pulled her as if to hug her, but instead gave her a final shove. Off they both went onto the hard wooden floor.

"You idiot!"

"So what do you want to know, Mel?"

She hid her head under her arm. "I dunno," she whispered.

"Oh." He sat up and dusted himself off. "Tell you what, I've got a special delivery to make."

"Right."

He looked at her quizzically like a puppy with his head to one side. In a few moments he was gone, murmuring, "I missed you."

She watched out the window as he drove off with his cargo: a brass headboard adorned with white porcelain bells.

As soon as Ted left the cabin, Gladys started in. She flew into the bathroom, hopped over to the sink and proceeded to make a meal of a tube of lipstick Melie had left there.

"Spit it out!" Melie yelled, too late. The bird reacted to her squawking by flying dizzying circles around the cabin. Melie watched helplessly as a poop landed right in her open pocketbook. "Gross! First birdseed in my coffee. And now this. Ted was wrong. That was no accident. I'll get you back," Melie threatened, narrowing her eyes and trying to look as menacing as possible. "You better watch your back." Gladys just fluttered her feathers, but to Melie's eyes, she looked a little concerned.

With Ted out making his delivery, and Gladys making her own, Melie felt her best course of action was to go over to the Shoppe. Once there, she had a ball trying on his entire stock of antique clothing, crocheted shawls, evening gowns, dressing gowns, brooches, cameos, filigree pins, and accessories she termed "indeterminables." She settled on a mauve-colored satiny gown with a bell-shaped crinoline which she pulled over her own black leggings. Underneath a basket of old magazines, she unearthed a pair of low-heeled laced-up ivory boots. She hung a vintage brass teardrop necklace of gold and green around her neck. All that was missing was a suitable hat or feathers for her hair or maybe she should put her hair up in ringlets.

I could wear this splendid costume to the Victoriana Ball.

When she returned to the house, wearing a purple smock that went perfectly with her black leggings and black ballet slippers, she grabbed

Ted's heavy plaid shirt and slipped into it. The weather was turning a bit raw. Ted was home: puttering around outside, gluing, shoring up, stacking, sorting, but never throwing out. Later they sat on the deck out back watching the sun set over the forest behind the house.

Suddenly, Melie wanted to know something. "Do you think you could meet the 8:15 train on Friday?" She quickly took a bite of apple and stared down at her pretty little ballet slippers.

"LADY," roared the Baer, "we haven't met the train out here yet!" He stood up to his full height.

Melie jumped up at that and set her apple down on the step. She moved to the center of the deck and pulled the purple smock over her head, balling it up and throwing it into a corner.

"I'm ready to go. Could you get my suitcase?"

"Raring to go is more like it!" Ted swooped down on her and carried her through the house out the front door, across the road, and down the short path to the dusky lake. He stood her up like a big doll, held onto her, and stared into her big brown eyes. He pulled off her leggings and slippers.

"One for the road, milady?"

It felt like fifty degrees out this chilly evening, but . . .

"Oh, Ted."

Damn. I love it here!

On Friday, Melie was not on the 8:15, not having heard a word from Ted. One week rolled into two, then three. Everything was just a little too convenient for him . . . she was too convenient.

She went about her leaden life. Lines from Shakespeare came to mind:

> "At lover's perjuries, they say Jove laughs."
> "I'll prove more true than those who have more cunning
> to be strange."

It was not an easy time. No longer could she trudge along in the mud, placing her feet in the hardened footsteps she had left behind the day before. She had veered off the path now and the line was neither straight nor smooth nor obvious nor easy.

She didn't want to give in to panic, yet . . .

CHAPTER IX

EVEN MORE DESPERATE MOVES

Melie had actually "met" one of Ted's kids back in April simply by picking up the phone while he was out on a business call.

"Don't let him fool you," Sheila advised.

Melie stopped fiddling with the crumbs on her breakfast plate. "How do you mean?"

"You'll soon see."

"No, wait." *Help me please, I don't see,* she wanted to cry out.

After a pause, Sheila inquired, "What was it you wanted to ask?"

"No, nothing. That's fine. I'll tell Ted—your father—you called." Melie put the ivory antique phone back into its cradle.

I don't know this girl, she reminded herself.

"Ted, Sheila wants to meet me," Melie had said when he returned to shower and get ready for dinner.

"Sheila? Did she call up today? What does she want?"

"I already told you."

"But she didn't know about you when she rang . . ."

"She didn't? I just assumed—

"No, we've not very close anymore."

"How sad. When did you last see her?"

"Lunch on Tuesday."

"Tuesday?" *The day Doug got that look on his face. A call that day would have been nice.*

Ted seemed to be studying Melie out of the corner of his eye. He opened his mouth to speak but seized upon the first distraction at hand: Gladys clamoring for attention. Ever the indulgent parent, he bounded up, stretched, flashing a wicked Jack Nicholson smile at Melie.

"What's gotten into my girl now?" he cooed as he took Gladys out of her cage.

Don't let him fool you, Melie thought.

"Sheila'll be by for her annual visit one of these days," he shouted from the other room.

"Uh-huh. When?"

Ted seemed not to hear her. "You'll get along fine. Sheila's a whip. Like her mom."

"And me?"

"You ain't exactly chopped liver, lady," he said, sneaking up behind her and licking the area between collarbone and neck. "More like *paté.*"

That was when? Five months ago. And she hadn't been there when Sheila stopped over on her day off, a Tuesday. Why was Ted keeping them apart? Time to see now what clues Sheila could give her. She picked up the phone.

Melie entered the coffeehouse she had chosen a good distance from her office and spotted Sheila easily. She must have been five foot eight, with Ted's big build, honey-colored hair, and his eyes. Hers were a pretty blue. She was wearing a white lab coat, befitting a dental technician, which she was, and cradling a hot chocolate.

"Thanks for meeting me," Melie said as she slid into the booth.

"I was curious about you too."

She's a little more forthright than her dad. Melie signaled the waitress to bring her a cappuccino.

Sheila started right in. No small talk for her. "My dad had a hard life."

"So, tell me something I don't know."

(Silence). Sheila crossed her arms across her chest and clamped her mouth shut.

"Sorry, Sheila."

"I thought you're a social worker or something? Trained to listen . . ."

"I said I was sorry. It's been a tough week." *Isn't it always?*

Sheila looked out the window for a few moments, then resumed talking. "Dad's not like you. No degree. His father drove a cab. His mother died when he was only eleven."

Melie gratefully sipped the cappuccino the waitress brought over. "Was he close to her?"

"Very! Ask him about the stories she told him after school. Her beautiful singing voice. The green perfume bottle on her dresser . . ."

"Wait! Are you sure? Green?"

"You're interrupting!" Sheila protested, sounding a lot younger than her years.

Melie waited for her to continue.

"Grandpa was, frankly, a bit of a low-life, conning money, cigarettes and booze at the local bar. Lots of booze. Grandma, all together different. She held things together by typing papers for students at Queens College. When Dad and my mom, Sally, got together, Mom got pregnant right away. Dad tried to make the best of it. Soon I came along and there were four of us living in a cramped basement apartment in Brooklyn, surrounded by cement except for a patch of dirt out back where my brother and I played."

Sounds like my basement apartment. "Why are you telling me all this?"

"Just listen, okay?" Sheila insisted. "Dad started driving upstate on weekends to see what was there. Finally he found a spot he wanted to live in, a village in the mountains—where he's sitting right now. He started dragging us all up there every weekend for camping and rowing and fishing and stuff."

"A nice escape?"

"Ha! Not really. Mom hated the country. She invented reasons for us not to go. Sore throats and such. We started staying behind and then, you know . . ."

"No, what?"

"Mom started hanging out with her continuing ed professor, and one-two-three, we found ourselves moved in with him. Had to adjust to life in the suburbs. And a new daddy." Sheila sat back in her chair and took a sip of her cocoa. "That was when I was five—about twenty years ago."

"Hmm. I see." Actually, Melie didn't. See at all. She glanced at her watch quickly, holding her arm under the table, but not quickly enough. Sheila's face clearly telegraphed her annoyance.

"He was trying to do right by us kids and Mom. I realize that now." Sheila said loudly.

"Go on."

"He's become sort of a wooly and wild man, tinkering with machines, buying more and more of other people's stuff, out in the woods too, taking photos of nature and animals. Oh—and that stupid parrot!"

Melie took a deep breath and thought about whether to ask the next question. Oh, what the hell! "It's a macaw . . . . Sheila, what about women? Has he had many "involvements" with other women since your mother left? He must get lonely. You know what I mean."

"According to Helen Call, Finn Lake's resident town gossip, sometimes he invites ladies who are up skiing for the weekend into his bed. Oh, the image—I try not to think about it!" said Sheila, grimacing. Then she added, "Sorry."

"Hmm."

"I don't get the impression these "involvements" are ever really serious. All he tells me is that most of these women are godawful snobs and way too citified for him."

"Meaning?"

"Honestly, Melie, I'm not sure. He may be saying that just to protect himself. But I wouldn't be surprised if he were getting it on with Helen herself! I definitely got that impression once—"

"Stop Sheila," Melie held up a hand. "TMI." Melie asked the waitress for a second cappuccino. She sat back in her seat to reflect on what Sheila had said. Amazing how people, strangers, would lay their whole life stories bare on the table before her. *The seamstress, Helen Call?!*

"You know I almost forgot. There was this grade school teacher that he hung out with for a long time, a couple of years, back in the eighties. When he came into the city to visit me and Joe, he sometimes brought her along. She was kinda kooky but okay, I guess. He was pretty taken with her, for a time anyway."

"What happened?"

"Something terrible. She was walking to her car after school and . . . What do you call it when your brain explodes?"

"She had an aneurysm?"

Sheila nodded. "I think he took that very hard." Sheila paused then leaned forward and spoke softly. "Melie, he likes you. He's told me about the improvements you've made in his Shoppe. He kinda chuckles when he mentions you. I'm just worried that he doesn't know how to have a girlfriend. I can tell you'd be good for him."

Melie smiled and reached out to pat Sheila's hand. "Thank you for sharing that." After a few more minutes, she told Sheila she really needed to get back to work. She paid the bill, grabbed her blazer, and put out her hand to shake Sheila's when Sheila surprised her with a hug. *A Baer hug. Runs in the family.*

Sheila's parting words to her were: "A good man like my father doesn't come along every day. Ha. I oughta know. I've had a string of losers myself. Some day when you have more time. . ."

Replaying their conversation on the walk back along York Avenue, Melie realized she might have to go on the attack, fight for her man, her life. First, that damn parrot. Then she'd have to see about other possible female rivals.

Melie rode the train into the city one morning opposite a beaky young woman with red green yellow plumage. Melie stared through a dirty window into the drab outside world, keeping an eye out for unexpected moves from her seatmate, sudden fits or flights, unsolicited spite.

Gladys-Woman sharpened her claws on a thin board kept on her body for that purpose, then reddened them with a brush. She seemed almost ready for action. She pulled on her straggly brown feathers, sticking strands one by one into her beak to clean them with beads of her own sticky saliva. She was completely absorbed in her task.

Melie looked out the window. "Fire with fire," she mumbled. Getting up as the train pulled in, she lost her balance and half fell on the woman.

"Sorry." Melie could see she had smudged the Gladys-Woman's nails. "Really!"

The woman waved her hands menacingly in the air. "You bitch!" she screamed.

No one even looked up from their newspapers.

On the crosstown walk to work, Melie stopped at a drugstore counter.

"Two bottles of Amazon Red, please. And make that a matching lipstick to go."

It had been almost a month since she'd spent a weekend upstate and learned that Ted didn't "do" relationships. She'd held out long enough.

Late Friday afternoon Melie flew to Finn Lake on one of those upstate six-seat puddle jumpers, thinking about her meeting with Sheila, and had no trouble hailing a cab in her new navel orange v neck shift. When she paid the driver, her green-grape bracelets jingled on her wrist, the green silk belt tightened suggestively around her small waist, hiking her skirt up way over her knees, and her two big purple eggplant earrings swung slowly and pendulously around her face.

She paused before entering the Shoppe for a last minute check of her face and person. Pulling out her pocket mirror, she applied a bit more Amazon Red lipstick, and proudly inspected her painted nails (painted green!) and her toes peeking through the tops of her new white leather sandals.

"Ready for combat," she declared and pushed her way through the door. *Will Ted take the bait?*

He started squawking as soon as he laid eyes upon her. "Hey, is that my Chiquita Banana come to visit? C'mere, gorgeous!" He rushed out from behind the counter to swoop her into his arms.

Channeling her best Mae West imitation, she crooned, "Is that a pistol in your pocket . . . or are you just glad to see me?"

Ted wasted no words. He locked up and dragged her into the back room, but not before she spotted Gladys, fuming in her corner, taking mini steps back and forth, finally retreating to the safety of her cage.

Never underestimate the resourcefulness of a good HR manager.

Many hours later, after a lovely evening of homemade delights, culinary and otherwise, at about three AM . . .

Melie retreated to her hiding place behind a tall oak as Ted flew out of the cabin half dressed, screeching, "Gladys, Gladys-Baby, what has she done to you?"

Gladys responded by continuing to jump from tree branch to tree branch around the perimeter of the cabin. She was unaccustomed to the great outdoors, and making enough racket for the soundtrack of a PBS Special on the Amazon Jungle.

Melie hissed, "Shut up, Gladys," hoping to drown out the bird's anguished cries.

So intent was Ted on scanning the trees beyond for a sight of Gladys in the dim light, he apparently never saw her heavy red wrought-iron cage, parked just a few yards from the open door. He tripped and went down hard.

"That lousy tourist," he muttered. He lay spreadeagled on the grass in only a pajama top, shivering as the predawn mist fell on his bare legs.

Melie guffawed in spite of herself. *I bet he's showing the moon a face it hasn't seen since 1956, when he tumbled out of the back seat of his Dodge with Sally Anne McDonough to joyously consummate six months of lustful teenage licking, petting, and pawing.*

That little "involvement" did not turn out so well in the grand scheme of things, she thought, though Sheila and her brother were bound to feel differently.

"This is just ridiculous," he cried. "What are you doing?" He propped himself up on one elbow. Melie, out of breath, emerged from behind a tree, waving an oversized butterfly net around. "Where'd you get that?"

"Never mind." *I got a buyer on Craigslist lined up and I'm not about to disappoint.* But she needed to take a breather. Gladys was a lot bigger, faster and perhaps smarter than a butterfly, and definitely faster than Melie, and Melie was having a tough time trapping her. "Ted, face it. Gladys is the Alpha Female in this household. I'm an intruder. This has got to stop." Melie propped the net against a tree and started rolling a boulder over in the direction of the cabin, not knowing what she was going to do with it.

"Melie . . . let's talk here a minute. This is getting a little out of hand."

"Don't worry. It's not for you. It's for your precious love," she sneered. She felt as if she had been stuck in the spin cycle of her old washing machine—her short, black curls were wet and plastered flat against her face, and her thin jointless arms and legs were jerking to a tune heard only in her head. But she was gaining fast on the cage. She checked on Gladys. The bird was giving Ted the eye and hopping up and down on a high branch of the tree nearest the cabin. Get me out of this, now! she seemed to plead. *Forget it, little one. You're mine.*

Ted grabbed his left elbow and said in a low voice, "Ow, I think I sprained something bad." He sat back on his haunches and looked up at Melie imploringly.

"Too bad, Ted, too bad. You shoulda thought of that before." She rolled the heavy boulder closer.

"Before what?" Cradling his left elbow, he asked, "Exactly what did I do to you, lady?"

"You don't know?"

"Afraid I don't. I didn't take your advanced college courses on human sexuality, you see." Then he sneezed.

Melie jabbed her finger at Gladys who was taking in the whole scene with her two coal black beady eyes, advancing and retreating along the length of a dirty besplattered tree branch, beak ready for action, looking like nothing less than the first-ever twentieth century parrot-woman gladiator. Every time the parrot heard Ted's voice, her squawks rose an octave or two.

Melie looked at Gladys, then him, hesitant, resting the boulder under her foot. She pushed damp hair off her forehead. *It's just a bird.*

"Take a deep breath, lady."

She followed his advice. "She's really spooked, isn't she?"

"C'mon, Melie, come look at my arm."

She knelt down beside him. He stroked her face with his good hand. "Don't worry now. You can bandage it for me. It's just a sprain."

Without warning, he lunged at her then, pinning her to the wet gravel. He managed to kiss her, and she kissed him back before she bit him in the cheek.

"Owwww!" He rubbed his cheek, wide eyed, forgetting about the elbow.

"I'm sorry," she mumbled, "I don't know why . . ."

Ted narrowed his eyes as if she were starting to seriously scare him. "Look, let's go in. Gladys must be getting quite a chill. Aren't you, baby?"

"DAMN THAT FUCKING BIRD!" Melie sprang to her feet. "She's getting it now. First I have to make love, listening to her watch me and knowing what she's thinking about my thighs and my butt and my breasts, and now . . . now. . . .I gotta get rid of her, Ted. Don't you see?" An idea came to her. "Can't we just let her fly away home?"

"South America? C'mon, calm down. Be reasonable. I like your breasts."

"I mean it." Her voice was very still. "I know how to take care of my detractors."

"Okay, okay, look, I'll catch her and put her in the shed for now."

"Ted, face it. She's. . . interfering. I don't know how your other girlfriends could stand that evil bitch, those eyes."

"What other girlfriends?" Ted mumbled. "Do you mean Helen Call? Did Sheila tell you something?"

"Oh . . . .Ted, this is your last chance, our last chance."

"You got that right," he muttered. He stood up, walked over to the tree, and held out his arm. Gladys immediately hopped from branch to branch to branch. Landing on Ted, she rubbed her cheek against his. He dragged the cage behind him and ushered her into the shed, making a few discreet tsk tsk noises along the way.

Melie did not dare to move. He emerged from the shed and approached her slowly. "Gonna fix my arm up, lady?" She nodded weakly. They stumbled together through the front door, his good arm around her neck, her hand on his bare butt.

Saturday passed quietly. Gladys would only reluctantly leave the security of her cage and cowered when Melie was in the vicinity. Ted devoted extra time to Gladys, tickling and cajoling her. Later Melie and Ted went out fishing for a few hours. Melie felt ragged and worn out. By early afternoon she told Ted she had things to do in her apartment and did not know when she would see him next. He drove her to the airport in silence.

Upon returning from work a few nights later, Melie opened up an envelope and unfolded sheets of notebook paper with almost illegible scribble covering both sides. She had no idea who would write to her until she spotted the first sentence:

> Let me introduce myself: Theodore Baer ("Ted" to my
> drinking buddies and of course "Teddy Bear" to all the
> girls). I started life, you could say, as pretty much of a

93

fuckup, drinking in the afternoons with Pa, getting my first girl, Sally, knocked up when we were sixteen, and having to drop out of high school to get married.

Maybe if I hadn't lost my mother when I was so young—she was hit by a drunk teenager while crossing a street—things might have been different. I'd probably have shaped up a lot sooner. She was a real lady: quiet and always reading poetry. She had a lovely voice I can still hear. She gave me lots of good advice about how to handle the school bully or how to ask a girl, actually Sally, to the junior high school prom.

Ma liked old things and spent a lot of time up in the attic, going through boxes of stuff. So you see where I got it from!

My childhood? I never went anywhere except to play cards or shoot craps or look at porno postcards with the other kids in an empty garage. And guess whose cards they were?

I decided to make the most of it when Sally got pregnant though it was mostly her sloppiness. We moved to a one-room flat in a two-family house her aunt owned in the Bronx. I got a job in Sales—I had inherited the gift of gab from Pa. People took a liking to me so I did all right. I always was a good-looking specimen with my manly build, hair that was reddish blond in those days, hazel eyes (wink). Luckily, Mom had taught me good English and I sounded like I had an education, though I didn't.

I had no time to spend with my family but I was determined to get my kids off the mean streets. When I was thirty, I found a spot I wanted to live, a village in the mountains. Did I know how Sally felt about the country? I wound up alone in Finn Lake. The last thing I wanted. Twenty years ago.

Now I might look like a crusty old man, running this huge antique business, like I been here forever. I get to go to town and assemble all sorts of junk that people seem to love. I tinker with old machinery and look at pictures and magazines of how people used to live. I go fishing on the lake at least twice a week and I've cut down on my drinking, but I go to town just the same.

Now you know a while back I repaired an old camera, and I have to say I've taken some pretty decent photos. You've seen them. Sometimes, ha! I admit I use them to lure lonely ladies from New York City into my Victorian bed in the back room. They think I'm quaint. (Sound familiar?)

I don't say what I think of them.

It's a solitary life but I got Gladys. I bought her from a guy, a breeder, right after my divorce. I didn't want to stay up here by myself. Gladys, I admit, is a pip and a pain—like all women, I guess! But you have to understand she's been there for me when I had no one.

I would have to say I'm pretty casual about how I care for things, but there's only me and Gladys to please. Simple. I have my small pleasures and get involved in town events, like Victoriana, and even politics just a bit to get out some. Of course I get into New York City once in a while, maybe twice a year, to check on Sheila. I heard you two met. I always knew you'd get along. Did I ever tell you my boy Joe is working on oil rigs in Alaska?

My goal in life? To share what I love about nature with a woman I can love. One who's not too into herself and too citified. But I'm not educated and all I have to offer is good country sex, my extra special pancake Sundays, and . . . who knows?

You must wonder why I'm writing. I feel awkward talking about myself this way, but Sheila ordered me to do it! She said to tell you I'm not a saint, I've done bad, even since I've known you. (Sorry.) It's true. But I'm ready to stop now.

So, I never really asked about your family, Melie. Anything you can share with me? Nothing too shocking please. I don't have your sophisticated apparatus for taking things in. Ha!

Melie, all I really want to know is one thing: When are you coming back? (Don't give up on me.)

Yours, Ted.

P.S. I promise to put Gladys in the shed when we you-know!

P.P.S. I guess things are tough for you right now? I know you'd never hurt another living creature. . . .

Melie never thought Ted would write to her like this, especially after she launched that botched attack on Gladys and him. Surely that should have been enough to scare anyone off? She'd only wanted to capture Gladys, not kill her, and spirit her away somewhere safe and warm and far far away. She reread the letter, experiencing a rush of pleasure, but not for long.

Now she'd have to tell him about her parents, whom she'd nicknamed Minos and Rhadamanthus, Greek judges of the underworld, eternally judging her; what it was like to hear Dad say that he never wanted a child; he only did it to please Mom. And Mom who paraded her around in starchy collars and frilly dresses, and told people, "Look, my daughter is much prettier than me," all the while waiting for the protestations. Mom (and Dad?), competing with her all their lives, never letting her breathe.

They had never been on her side, and they were as good as dead and buried, playing shuffleboard and canasta in some God's-Waiting-Room village on the east coast of Florida.

She reread the letter. This was what she wanted, wasn't it? Yet . . . Confused, she grabbed a sheet of paper off her desk and drew two columns, plus and minus. She had tried this particular technique before with men, wanting to be brutally honest and bottom line, but somehow she always tried to hang on too long or was tempted to let go too quickly. Making a list was a rational thing to do; dreaming the dreams she dreamt at night was not. Yet both usually (almost always) told the same story.

Is Ted the Right Man for Me?

[+]	[-]
Handsome, sexy, available	Could lose a few lbs.
Funny	Predictable.
Knows about things I know nothing about	Not as smart as me—is he?

[+ or -?]

Ted is not a bit like anyone I have ever met. And he's unflappable.

Travelling on weekends could not go on. She had exhausted most of her small savings account. She was tired too. He had offered to come down and see her once or twice, but for some reason she was not comfortable with the idea of him, his large feet planted in her basement living room, his ampleness fitting into a corner of the too-soft sofa, his wild mop of hair just inches from the artificially-lowered ceiling.

And could that lumberman jacket of his be wrapped around a chair in the window of a café on York Avenue? *Omigod, what a snob I'm turning into.*

He and her friends, her staff. They wouldn't understand. He might undermine her reputation at Axis Mundi Medical Center. Yes, she was sure of it. They would know she was just a woman after all, capable of feeling what they felt. Dangerous. No, she could not allow that to happen. He had to stay where he was.

Still, she carefully folded up his letter, reinserted it into the envelope, and slid it under her pillow, hoping for sweet dreams.

However that night's dream was anything but sweet.

I'm with a woman in a hotel. I've killed two men or wounded them and put them in a suitcase. I press buttons to close the suitcase, and put it in the closet. I feel sorry about one of them, like him. I go out to dinner and hesitate between being hungry for a hamburger and being unable to eat.

I ask my friend if she has important papers in the hotel—must we go back there? Can we run away? She says no.

Melie, in a half-awake state, tried desperately to resolve the action. Couldn't she call the police to go to the hotel? But what would people think of her? How could she explain this to everyone she knew—that she had committed the worst crime there is? Murder! And she had no clue as to how or why.

She jumped out of bed and splashed cold water on her face. Staring into the bathroom mirror she had an epiphany: she needed desperately to meet *her*. Once, she had caught a glimpse of her during a yoga meditation: a small face framed by short curly white (!) hair, the knowledge that this was the essence of her, the way other people would see her. No face paint, no hair dye, just herself in the center, there.

It was time they met. The Dreammaster kept sneaking her in disguised as twins, as mothers, brothers, daughters, sisters, murderesses. There was always the same thing happening in her dreams these days: violence and violations, intrusion, the burn to escape, to save her life. She was going to die, be killed, or she killed and made die! It was getting pretty tedious. It was getting old. She needed a breakthrough already.

She backed away from the mirror and padded into the kitchen to make some herbal tea, and slowly get ready for a new day. She reminded herself that she'd better start focusing on her work or she'd be swept under by cascading crises.

"What are you saying, Dr. Tamis?" Melie asked again, but again forgot to listen for the answer. Every year she came for her annual exam; why should this year be any different? She glanced at her wrist—she'd forgotten to put her watch on that morning. She stood up to peek through the door at the clock in the hallway.

"Blah, blah, blah" was all she heard.

"I have to get back to work now. It's two already." Melie sat down again on the end of the examining table and wondered why Tamis was looking at her that way. He put a hand on her shoulder and squeezed. God, she hated that! Shouldn't he know better by now, after all their talks?

The intercom buzzed. He took the call, shook his head, and left. She retrieved her clothes from the hook on the back of the door and hastily reassembled herself. There wasn't even a mirror there for the patients.

At the registrar's desk, a newbie asked her what time tomorrow did she want to set up the biopsy. "I'll give you a call," she said and left the building. The rain was coming down in sheets.

Was that Lucille she saw walking toward her? People said she disappeared from her desk for hours at a time. Doing what? Walking around the medical campus? Delivering mail? Maybe it was just someone who looked like Lucille. Melie put up her umbrella and darted around the corner in the direction of her office. No time for lunch—people by now were probably taking numbers and lined up by her door, seeking salvation. She was in a mood to dispense it, all right.

CHAPTER X

THE CENTER CANNOT HOLD

What Melie had long dreaded occurred. Doug Milty summoned her to his office in D Building. Death. Doom. Dereliction of Duty.

"I see, Ms. Kohl, that Lucille is still at her desk. It's been *months* since I ordered you to send her away."

"—"

He noisily cleared his throat.

"Doug, Mr. Milty, you cannot just force an employee out on disability. And no one knows that better than Lucille, the records manager in charge of all paid time off. Let me read you a few recent court decisions to remind you of Axis Mundi Medical Center's liability should said employee decide to sue us for discrimination based on disability or presumed disability."

She did just that while he stared at a point between her breasts. Her dress was zipped to the max, almost choking off her air supply.

He interrupted. "Come over here," he said gruffly.

Melie sat further back in her chair. "What is it?" she asked.

"I said, get over her, Mel!"

"No. No, I don't think I will." Her eyes darted around the room searching for a way out.

"Let's put it this way. We're talking in this room which is not bugged, presumably. I am your senior in every way, and in fine fettle with the Dean of Axis Mundi, who by the way just became my brother-in-law."

"Oh, Lord."

"I want to share something with you now."

"I don't get your drift, Doug." Melie, sensing a change in the weather, shot straight out of her seat.

"Then just get this." He stood up too, still not looking directly at her, and pulled down his pants zipper. Out popped Mr. Schlong, all pink and powdery, about the size of a half piece of chalk.

"You get this in your mouth in five seconds flat, sister, and make me rise like a loaf of sourdough bread, or you'll be buying dog food this time next week!"

He was attempting to grab it between his thumb and index finger while he spoke. "That is, if your food stamps stretch that far."

Melie slowly approached his desk. "Doug, have you ever been treated at Axis Mundi for micropenisia? 'Cause I think I detect a small problem . . ." With that, Melie grabbed a heavy IRS tome off the edge of his desk and raised it above her head. "And I know just what to do about it."

"Hey now. Back off, will you!" He turned around and zipped his schlingy-schlong back in, then faced her.

She dropped the heavy tome onto his desk. "I really do not need this right now, Doug," she said slowly and tonelessly as she backed out of his office. "And neither do you." She hoped that sounded threatening. She turned and ran. No witnesses about. There were never any witnesses. Just where was his Annabelle, his assistant?

Sukie and Geena piled into Melie's office as soon as she returned from accounting. Melie guessed she was looking rather disheveled. Shaken. Breathless.

Even before they closed the door behind them, Sukie dared to ask, "What happened between you and Milty? How did it go? Something's the matter—"

"I cannot discuss it." Melie plopped down, exhausted, in her chair.

Geena put on a knowing smile. "Oh no—don't tell me you slept with him?"

Melie glared at her. "GEENA!"

The three women looked at each other and then away.

Melie spoke up. "Let's just say we came to a little arrangement."

Sukie sat forward in her seat. "We're hanging on every world, Mel."

Geena cut to the chase. "Spill the beans!"

At this very opportune moment, Arielle buzzed in. "Melie, Babs is out here. She's kinda hysterical."

Melie tilted her head towards the door. "Everybody out of my office. Now! And send Babs in."

"My therapist says I fall apart when I'm not working, and I'm not working now."

Melie was sitting next to Babs once again, with her arm around the woman, passing her tissues, patting her shoulder, and occasionally squeezing it as Babs cried her heart out, all things Melie was probably not adequately paid for, if paid for at all, when Arielle buzzed in again.

Both women jumped. "What, Arielle?"

"Doug Milty's on the line. He said to interrupt you, whatever."

"No."

"Yes, he actually said that."

"I know, but he can't." Melie slammed her hand down on her desk for emphasis. Babs jumped.

"What's going on?" Babs inquired, pulling at Melie's sleeve.

Arielle sighed. "What do you want me to do?"

"I cannot come to the phone now."

Ten minutes later, a breathless Arielle rang in, "Doug's out here and..."

Next thing he was pounding on the door with both dimpled fists. "Let me in, Melie, goddamit!"

Babs perked up. "Who put a carrot up his tush?" she asked. "You know, Mel, I always thought he had a thing for you."

Melie put a finger to her lips and tried to figure out what to do. She looked for a fingernail to nibble on, but alas, they had all been taken. She got up and paced. Then she walked back to the desk and put her hands on Babs's shoulders. "You're not so bad, Babs."

"Yeah, that's what my therapist keeps telling me."

Just then, Doug let out a roar: "M E L I E!"

"Let's see how good you really are, kid." Melie quickly whispered instructions in Babs's ear.

"Coming," called Melie, merrily, as she clicked open the door.

Doug barged in, shirt hanging out of his pants, jacket sleeves rolled up, sweat beading on his pink pork roast forehead. He was bellowing, "WHAT THE HELL, WOMAN?"

"Barbara Freedman is a medical secretary here and she's not having a good day," Melie said, pointing to a pair of Keds sneakers, heels in the air, poking out from under her desk.

"What gives?"

"How do I know?"

"Hey, you're the damn crisis manager!"

"Yes, but I confess I don't know what to do in this case. I promise to think about it over lunch." And at that, Melie beat a swift retreat out of her office past Arielle in Reception where she could still hear Doug Milty pleading with Babs.

"C'mon, Ms. Freedman, get outta there. Pl-ee-se!"

"Noooo," Babs moaned in response.

When Melie returned two hours later, she found Babs fast asleep, still sprawled under the desk.

"You can get up now." Melie stood over Babs, waiting for her to reemerge.

"Nah."

"*Now!*"

"Please Mel, don't yell. Honestly." Babs pulled herself up, not bothering to dust off, and plopped into the nearest chair. She studied Melie's face, actually reaching out and touching her red lips. "What're we going for here? Maybe you ought to try a subtler effect?"

"No. I like it," Melie responded. She pulled out her compact mirror and reapplied a fresh coat of lipstick. "It suits me."

"Hey, Mel, how's that guy doing—the one upstate?"

"Oh, I don't know, Babs." Melie sat in the other visitor chair and put her head down on the desk, moaning softly.

"Tell Dr. Babs everything."

While she unburdened herself, she let Babs take all incoming calls, even handling a mini-crisis with Dr. Tamis, who was at least learning to question some of his actions.

"Oh, Dr. T.," Babs said, "I don't think that would be appropriate, do you? Be honest now."

Ah, that's how you do it.

Mid-afternoon, the intercom buzzed. Melie was alone in her office, having convinced Babs that her work was done for the day.

"*She's* out here."

"Damnitall! Coming. . ." Melie walked out to greet Resident Psycho, the same who had once put her hands around the neck of Melie's predecessor and raised her up about two feet from the ground. So far Melie had been luckier, but she found this woman frightening nonetheless.

"Did you make an appointment to see me?"

"Melie! They're closing the lights on me again. I wrote up what they're doing to me— they don't know I'm listening." She shoved a two inch wad of yellowed papers at Melie.

Melie didn't touch the papers and let them fall to the floor. "Make an appointment and we'll discuss it. Understand?"

Resident Psycho jabbed her three times on the shoulder.

"Don't do that!"

"You know, Melie? They're not right. What they're doing to you . . ."

Melie nodded. Then she noticed Resident Psycho smiling. *Shit! Now she thinks I'm on her paranoid schizophrenic side! The EAP director told me never to nod at people like her. So I got away again with the appointment farce and I blew it anyway.*

"You need an appointment to see me. Then I'll be glad to discuss the situation." Melie returned to her office, chewing on a dried-out cuticle. Amazingly, this tactic had been working for some time as Resident Psycho did not have the executive planning ability to schedule her meltdowns in advance. Unlike Melie.

The next two up to bat were the Employee Who Wouldn't Sit Down and the Employee Who Wouldn't Stand Up. Melie stood with the first; she'd flattened herself out and crawled under the coffee table in Reception to pull the second out. The first employee, poor thing, suffered from paranoid delusions caused by a case of advanced Lupus (according to her supervisor/doc); the second was breaking down, understandably, because her teenage son had just been admitted to Axis Mundi's psych ward, and she couldn't pay her rent without the income he brought in from selling drugs to the suits from the suburbs.

It was all understandable, wasn't it? If you screwed up your ears to hone in on the distant subterranean grinding of the earth's tectonic plates as they slid past each other, you wound up hearing all the explanations you would ever need. In this world at least...

Lucille dropped in late afternoon as Melie was writing up her notes on the day. For her to visit was unprecedented.

"How's it going, Lucille?" Melie asked cautiously.

Lucille just stared at a point above Melie's head. Melie turned to look, but could see nothing riveting about the hospital-green wall which was overdue for a paint job by about ten years. She turned back. "I know it's been hard on you," she began, noting Lucille's beautifully manicured nails had recently been reduced to ragged stumps. She thought she should get right to the crux of the matter. "Lucille, are you feeling perhaps that you need to take some time off?"

"You'd like that," Lucille shot back, giving her a look worthy of Gladys.

"What?" Melie was taken aback but she tried another tack. "Look we've never been chummy, but as employee relations manager, I feel I should point out—"

"Shut your hole! I've got your number, Melanie Kohl!"

"I see you're not ready to discuss this topic," Melie continued as sweat beaded on her forehead, "but—"

The intercom rang and Melie lunged for the phone. "Who is it? Sukie? Sukie is upset? I'll be right out." She looked up to see Lucille had taken a powder. *Now what was that about?* she wondered. She ventured out of her office—a mistake—and found Sukie, sobbing at her desk, surrounded by forms in triplicate and empty teacups. "What is it, Sukie?"

Melie presented her tired listener's face and tried to absorb Sukie's tale of woe. "Sukie, listen," she said, sitting down in the victims' chair. "Your mom needs to be in a nursing home. Now. She almost burned your apartment down. She's not eating. She's ninety-seven."

Sukie nodded and dabbed at her eyes.

"Let me help you fill out all the papers."

When she finished with Sukie, it turned out Arielle needed attention too. Melie took her back into her office and got Geena to cover the desk. Listening to Arielle's lament, she reached certain conclusions.

"Your boyfriend's a bigot." Melie repeated patiently.

106

"How can that be? He's Jewish and I'm Jewish."

"But he's not respecting the fact that you want to keep a kosher home. He's bringing unkosher hot dogs in. Making fun of you. Saying you'll need two kitchens if you live together."

Arielle said nothing but appeared puzzled.

"Amazingly, Arielle, it's just not going to work!" Once again, Melie had fixed the problems of others. She was feeling rather smug and stopped by Geena's office.

Geena, per usual, was sitting in her office, chatting on the phone which she obligingly put on hold. "What's up, boss-lady?"

"Geena, good time last night?" Geena had had a blind date opportunity the night before.

"Not ankles-in-the-air good time. But he was nice enough I guess."

Omigod, I am so old, Melie thought. Geena's phone was beeping; the person on hold no doubt impatient. Melie said simply, "I see."

A few minutes later, as she was packing up to leave for the day, Melie noticed a handwritten scrap of paper stuck to a corner of her blotter:

Hands off Dr. Tamis!

I wonder what that's all about.

During the evening commute, Melie was on watch. She studied the man sitting opposite.

The silver-haired gent grimaced as if his belly were on fire. An antacid couldn't touch this one. His smile was all wrong—wrong side up—and he seemed to gulp air and swallow saliva, hoping perhaps to reach the forest fire within with a few cooling droplets.

He picked up his paper to read, but his whole being continued to generate heat and unease that threatened to come at her in waves.

She turned away. Once, later, she glanced back. He held the paper at an angle, to his left, and bit down on his lip. Then he smiled in that pained way he had. She noticed he had not one briefcase, but two: one brown, one black leather, blown up to bursting point with briefs, newspapers, jottings and lists.

One button pulled tight across his paunch. Everything to do with him seemed ready to burst like an over-pumped bicycle tire or a child's balloon. All this power trapped and contained scared her—it was all too much like New York City and her life.

After Melie swallowed her dinner of yogurt mush—the added spoonful of raspberries failing to transform it into anything remotely sexy— she rocked back and forth in the black rocker. It was too early to go to sleep and she had completed all her nighttime rituals. She'd washed her dish and spoon and dried them and put them away. She'd finished her book on the train that morning, and no other reading material lying around the apartment promised to be gay and lighthearted and breezy and romantic. There was nothing on TV, not even a good Animal Planet special. Furryface was already deep under the covers and couldn't be counted on for a playmate. She had to face facts. She needed to call Ted. Victoriana was this weekend and she so wanted to go. He wanted her to go too in the worst way. But she'd lost that match with Gladys, though maybe she'd won? No, she couldn't quite believe that.

She crawled into bed with Furryface and curled up with her in a fetal position. *Too bad I gave up sucking my thumb when I was ten 'cause that would come in handy right now.*

That gave her an idea and she rushed out of bed to locate Oscar and plug him in. Good old dependable Oscar! How she longed to replace him, all of him. Could the next model come without a cord and no backup AA batteries? Maybe even have a face?

She went to work. *Ahhhhhh. . .*

But afterwards, her thoughts turned to Ted, sweet, kind, sexy Ted. She missed him so. Maybe she should have returned his calls? Answered his letter? Maybe Ted could still work out? No. No. Probably not. She had seen to that. *Good job, Melie.*

Now what?

Mid-morning a few days later Melie realized she hadn't seen much of Milty since the schlong incident. Unloading Babs on him—quite an effective deterrent. Like Merry Terry before him, he was not keen on setting aside a time each week to review her work, but he relented and said, "I want to see you in my office every Friday at four without fail."

Melie had managed to sidestep this issue by scheduling a crisis at exactly that time every week. "If you like, Doug," she'd offer, "I can bring the employee with me."

"That's not going to happen. I'm . . .busy. See you next week."

Once she'd admitted, "I'm working on a sexual harassment investigation and—"

"Fine," he'd said. "Don't involve me in that kind of thing." And he'd hung up.

Merry Terry would get incensed if she weren't brought up to speed on every last complaint. Melie's only option had been to run up and down the hall from Employment to Benefits (where Merry Terry had her office), dropping little notes like love letters on Merry Terry's desk. But Milty was in another building entirely. Running would not be practical, and she did not think he'd be much help anyway. Instead, he materialized from time to time like a bad dream out of the fog—

She first heard his thundering footsteps. Her door flew open and he poked his head inside. "The detectives want to see all the files Terry was working on, what she was up to on that background check project."

"Lucille—"

"Get her to make them available." He bore into her with his beady eyes and took one giant step forward.

Melie swallowed hard and put out a hand to stop him from entering her office. "Right away."

He looked her up and down, just because he could, turned and slammed out of her office.

Oh, no.

Melie ventured out into Reception, then quickly retreated when she spotted an overfed slightly sweaty frat boy squeezed into one corner of the black leather sofa, pretending to read *People Magazine.* She called her staff together for an impromptu meeting. "What are they up to now?" she asked. "If he's undercover, I'm Tokyo Rose." Sukie chuckled, the only one to get the reference of course.

Geena bounced in her seat, raising her hand, then dropping it and looking sheepish.

Oh Lord.

"That guy. He's been told to watch out for suspicious characters with difficult-to-fathom motives."

Make that two 'Oh Lord's.'

"Meaning," said Melie while turning to Sukie for confirmation, "that we too are included in this category."

Sukie piped up. "A better way to look at it, Melie—" She silenced herself. Melie was jiggling her right leg. "What I mean is—"

Arielle interrupted. "Melie? I just applied for a credit card. Will it be turned down now?"

Melie frowned and shook her head slightly, enough of a signal for Sukie to pick up on. "Arielle," she whispered, while patting her on the arm, "we'll talk about it later."

"One last question before we disperse," Melie said. "Have all the resumes and applications and background checks been turned over to the investigators?"

Sukie rose and shooed Arielle and Geena out the door before responding. "We have nothing to fear, Mel. We always keep good notes and documentation on all our hires."

Melie tapped her fingers on the desk.

"The answer is 'yes.' Lucille and the Records clerk pulled all the information and handed it over to them."

Melie nodded and mumbled thanks. She gestured to Sukie to exit and close the door. She stopped tapping and jiggling. Instead, she studied her nails, selecting a dry bit of cuticle for her chewing pleasure. The green nail polish had worn off long ago.

Lunchtime she ran into Carla from that voodoo-plagued department while buying coffee from the street vendor. Carla always seemed like potential friend material. They never lunched together, but enjoyed talking when they bumped into each other like this.

"I can't believe they still have yellow tape all over. I was kinda shocked when I went into Benefits to pick up an insurance form," Carla said.

"It's just around Terry's office." Melie had instructed her staff to steer clear of the area and to keep applicants far away so they wouldn't get "the wrong impression." *What a laugh!*

Melie still wondered that the media had not been more of a problem. Someone very high up in the Axis Mundi hierarchy had no doubt called in a few favors. News of Dean Terry's demise had been relegated to a back page of most newspapers, next to the prayers to St. Christopher, the meet-up's, the ads put in by those seeking to recover lost property. She didn't remember seeing anything on the television news channels beyond the initial reportage the day the body was discovered.

The general public remained clueless. Axis Mundi personnel continued to speculate for a bit but since no one actually missed Merry Terry . . . . One week the murderer was Dr. So-and-so who'd caught his wife and Merry Terry having a clandestine lesbian affair; the next, it was Arielle's boyfriend who wanted to scare her into resigning and giving up all hopes of a career, instead moving in with him. The saner staff joked about the others' gullibility or snidely remarked, "Don't they have any work to do?"

Even baby-faced Dr. Kohan was on the list of suspects, short and pudgy as he was.

Carla stepped closer to Melie and cautioned, "Melie, beware. If you are not careful, Axis Mundi will chew you up and spit you out."

"That'll take a pretty big maw and a lot of chewing. I've got a tough hide, you know."

Carla did not blink. They headed off in opposite directions with their muffins and drinks, drawn inexorably back to their desks by morbid curiosity and a compulsion to know what new hell awaited them.

After Carla's warning, Melie realized she ought to do something to neutralize Milty. That arrangement she'd alluded to, the one she actually did not have, she needed to have it. She decided to pay him a visit and stopped in at his office on her way home. He was sitting behind his desk, holding a magazine on his lap. Upon her entering his office, he tucked the magazine into a drawer and smiled. "Come in, Melie, and sit down. We have a lot of catching up to do."

Melie remained standing and started in on her rehearsed speech. "Milty, take a moment to reflect on the nature of my job. I know where all the bodies are buried."

"You know who offed Terry?" he asked, picking up his phone.

She gestured for him to hang up. "No, Milty. Maybe not that," she said, sensing she was losing him. "Well, a suspicion or two."

He was hooked again.

"I am privy to information not available to the general public. About people's education for one, their past employment history, and the truth of . . . certain rumors."

The color rose in his face and the expression morphed from shame to anger. "Wrap it up, you-who-know-too-much."

Melie hesitated. She hated to rely on his insecurities for her insurance. She watched as he thrummed his sausage-like appendages on the desk. As if summoned, his phone rang. He lunged for it and snarled, "Get out!"

She skedaddled, but not before saying, "I hope we understand each other."

So much for our little arrangement.

The phone rang at midnight. *Can't be anything good,* thought Melie, as she snapped awake and picked it up.

"Hello, Melie. I just want to let you know that Victoriana is this Saturday night, September 27, it's a big deal here, you need to see how incredible everything looks, and I'm . . .I'm expecting you to be my date." Ted said, all in a jumble.

"Ted?" She jumped out of bed, sent Furryface flying, and stood facing her newly-framed Pre-Raphaelite poster of two lovers crouching in a ruined garden. The male was leaning over the female, holding her gently, forever if he had to. The female was all pale skin, her eyes, limpid pools, her posture taut. She let herself be held but she knew this was not the end of their story. They still had dragons to slay and . . .

"Melie? Did you hear what I said?"

She feverishly smacked her cheeks with an open hand. "Yes. Ted. I'll be there. I will see you on Friday at eight-fifteen PM."

Ted let out his breath. Melie let out hers. Furryface leapt onto the bed and silently crept under the covers.

The Victoriana Ball! Melie was psyched at the prospect of strutting into the ballroom on Ted's arm, in full nineteenth-century regalia, like a latter-day Elizabeth Bennett. Maybe she'd even pirouette? What a chance to show off her pretty ivory laced-up boots!

"And aren't you a sight to behold," exclaimed Ted when she emerged from the bathroom to model her outfit. "That's the prettiest dress you've chosen, not too flouncy, just soft and feminine and pink—"

"Mauve," she corrected him. "And isn't this green stone necklace great?"

"You're great. I can't wait to tear it all off you," he added, lunging in her direction.

"Ted!" she said, positioning herself behind a chair.

"I guess I have to play nice. Time to go." He took another look at her. "Nice color combination, Melie. You should wear stuff like that more often."

Early Saturday evening, she and Ted strolled into Finn Lake's ballroom. *Wait. In the American Legion hall? Oh. Maybe this isn't going to be a Jane Austen night after all*, Melie thought.

The first thing Melie noticed was a tall medium-built woman in her late forties, rather pretty, in a pale apricot gown. A tiara of flowers held back ringlets of short frizzy red hair. Clearly the manager of the event, she held out dance cards to all the women as they entered. She offered one to Melie, then playfully grabbed it back as she took a moment to survey Melie from stem to stern.

"Helen Call, I presume?" Melie asked. "Bitch," she muttered under her breath.

Before Helen could respond, everyone's attention was diverted by the band tuning up onstage. Melie counted a couple of straggly-haired teenagers, one with a trumpet, the other on the drums, a guy, older than any hills she'd ever hiked on, flexing his accordion, and a lone woman with a beat-up violin. Folding chairs had been set out in a circle around the perimeter of the dance floor. *Good*, she thought, *I can always find a seat in the crowd of old ladies and not be too conspicuous.*

Helen broke up her reveries by tapping her on her shoulder with a folded up fan. Where was Ted? Melie quickly located him: he'd hightailed it over to the bar set up on the left side of the room. "You must be Melie. Right?" said Helen. "Didn't Ted tell you about dress conventions in Victorian days? That's a lovely mauve dress, but not for someone of your color and tone. Dark ladies never wore pink or pastels. You need color.

Here." Helen unwound a tiny artificial red rose from the plastic tiara wrapped around her head and placed it in Melie's hand.

"Oh, no, really," Melie protested.

Helen didn't hang around for thanks. She had moved on, spotting Ted across the room by the refreshments. She turned to add, "Next year you'll do better." Helen greeted Ted with a big smackeroo kiss on his lips. Melie felt blood turn to ice and all the color leaving her face. Her eyes sought out Ted's—but he was engrossed in deep and apparently soulful conversation with Helen and didn't look her way.

Be a grownup. She ensconced herself in a corner from which to observe the festivities. As she looked around, her cherished visions of channeling scenes from *Pride and Prejudice* were rapidly misting over. Instead of a spread of English puddings and *petits fours* sandwiches and colorful *crudités*, ham and fowl, trifle and jellies, this Victoriana Ball featured heaps of cold cuts and potato salad and coleslaw and pickles, albeit on beautiful china loaned from Ted's Shoppe. Instead of quadrilles and cotillions, scotch reels and two steps, they were more likely to be in for a rip-roaring polka. She hoped they had good wine and not just that beer favored by the locals. *No worries about overindulging tonight.*

But look—she already had her Darcy, a big bear of a Darcy. *If I'd only let myself believe that. . . .* Even after all the shenanigans she'd pulled, he still wasn't kicking her out from between the sheets. And he said in his letter he'd do better.

The band struck up a tune and couples gathered in the center of the floor to dance with their partners. Helen and Ted had seen to it that every woman in town was resplendent in a long silk, satin or chiffon gown adorned with rows of ruffles. Puffed sleeves showed off their delicate shoulders and *décolleté*, teased their beaux with peeks of rosy bosoms. Some had chosen high collars, the better to highlight their swan necks and long trains they could trail along the dance floor oh-so-gracefully to attract attention. Ted's young ladies looked exquisite. The swirls of color—peacock blue, champagne, maroon and deep purple, the whites and pinks and garnet greens—an impressionist painting come to life.

"I love your dress," said an aristocratic woman in red passing by. Melie looked down at her shiny mauve gown; she patted her upswept curls, threw the plastic rose in the corner, and pulled out a mirror to reapply some rouge and lipstick. She smiled to herself, a they-should-see-me-now smile, then, inevitably, started fretting. How could she keep up with Ted on the dance floor? She'd never danced a quadrille or cotillion or even a polka. She wasn't much of a dancer at all. Leonard the litigator had almost given up on her when he took her dancing on their first date and she stepped all over his new cowhide shoes.

"How many dances must I dance?" she asked Ted, biting her lip, when at last he joined her. He looked dashing in his dark grey dress coat, white vest, shirt and tie, and almost iridescent white patent leather boots.

"Melie, the custom is that couples dance the first dance together but otherwise do not dance with each other much. I know the ladies are counting on me to lead each of them to the dance floor for a fling. Aw, don't give me that New Yorker skeptical look. You know what I mean. We got widows and almost widows and young girls—"

"Almost widows?" Melie asked.

Just then the music started up, a polka. "Gotta run. I put my name on that young girl's card over there. Don't intend to disappoint." Ted bounded off across the floor. Then he backtracked, took her gloved hand in his, and raised it to his lips. "No monkey business, now. My love." She blushed down to her toes.

A boy, barely post pubescent, reached for her card and scribbled his name. "Let's do it," he said, as he swung Melie onto the dance floor but not before she caught the wink that passed from the boy to Ted.

Ah, he's got it all figured out, hasn't he?

Melie danced every dance that came up until the orchestra took a break. She'd read it was uncivil for a lady to refuse a man's offer to dance, and she certainly didn't want to embarrass Ted in any way. When the band stopped, she located Ted; he was in a crowd of his neighbors, reminiscing about something or other that had happened at a previous Victoriana Ball. She watched him and the faces of those following his story. He was the life of the party. She'd never seen him so gregarious. She preferred not to interrupt, sitting herself down instead at a stool near the makeshift bar for another cold beer. Who was standing next to her but Helen?!

Helen started in, "Melie, you look tired. Sweaty. Those poor ringlets you tried to twist your hair in, they're coming undone. Here, let me fix them for you."

Melie pulled away. "Don't trouble yourself," she said, perhaps too harshly.

Helen squinted at her for a second, then walked over to a gentleman in a wheelchair who she didn't bother to introduce.

Melie was still thirsty. She grabbed another beer and when she spotted Ted at the refreshment table, she eagerly jumped up to join him.

"I see you've met Helen and her husband, Sammy."

"Husband?"

"Sammy and I go way back, old fishing buddies. He used to be a professor at the community college. Sociology. A pity he had that stroke a few years ago. Let's go talk to them."

"Must we?"

He took Melie's hand firmly in his and led her to the circle of friends now surrounding Helen and Sammy. After a few pleasantries, the men stepped away to catch the score on the big screen TV downstairs, sticking her with Helen again.

"You got fire in your eyes, girl. Do you know that? But that's all right. Ted says you're smart, a little wacky. Well, a lot wacky. You leave that poor bird alone!" She wagged her finger. "You're certainly pretty though, and you don't look to be a runaround like his wife, Sally. He wouldn't make that mistake twice, not with me around." Helen grinned.

"You're full of compliments, aren't you?" Melie faced away from her, scanning the room for Ted.

"Listen, can I use you next year to breathe some new life into this ball? I mean, I got my hands full with altering the gowns for the young misses. Just look at those decorations. I'm sure a big city gal like you could do better than oak tag, balloons, and crepe paper. Pathetic, right? We need your help. What do you say?" Helen poked her arm to get her attention.

Melie, who never liked having her personal space breached, pushed Helen's arm roughly away and snarled, "Back off!" Desiring to put some distance between herself and this woman, and faced with limited options, she headed back to the bar for yet another beer. Ten minutes later when the music started up, an elderly man was staring in her direction and seemed destined to be her next partner. She was not in the mood for small talk and looked around, plotting an escape. She circled back to the Ladies Room she'd spotted near the front door and hid out in a stall for a bit.

Coming out of the stall, she banged right into Helen. Instead of excusing herself, she asked between clenched teeth, "Are you following me?"

Helen raised her eyebrows and gave her a quizzical look.

"Play that game if you want to," Melie responded. She retrieved her afro pick from her evening bag and attempted without much effect to draw it through her frizzed-out curls.

"Honey, you're killing that hairdo of yours. Why don't you let me help?" said Helen as she made a grab for the pick.

"I told you before—back off!" Melie, held out the pick in her right hand, pointed at Helen, and feinted a lunge. *Derrick the cook would be proud.*

Helen giggled. "Oh honey, get a look at yourself." Melie's eyes darted to the mirror. She let the pick fall to the floor. *Not too scary, am I? Maybe I should try out for a Victorian soap opera?*

The heroine's luscious chestnut curls tumbled suggestively down into her bodice. She was a vision in mauve, gold and green . . . but. . . she had treachery on her mind!

"Are you still there? Listen. You never answered me." Helen was a good six inches taller than Melie and looked like she could handle herself in a fight. Her hands were on Melie's shoulders. "Sit down on this stool a moment."

Melie's instincts kicked in, a little late in the game. *Got to defuse.* Melie obeyed.

Helen sat down next to her and took hold of one of her hands before continuing. "This is not how we act up here. I know you're upset with me. And Ted. Understand that after his stroke my husband, Sam, asked Ted to "look after" me, which he has done. Admirably. Now you're here." She waited for Melie to respond.

"Now I'm here," Melie repeated. She wrenched her hand away, turning to the sink to apply some hot pink lipstick and matching rouge. *Is it too much to ask for her to just disappear?* Catching Helen's eyes in the mirror though, she saw with surprise they were merry with mischief. *Helen Call cannot take a hint; Helen Call has no filter; Helen Call has been Ted's friend, and he hers, for years and they'd relieved each other's boredom. . . .I give up.*

Melie tucked her makeup back into her bag. She walked to the door, opened it, and turned back to Helen. "I'm not much of an artist but—"

"Done." Helen clapped. "Hurry. You don't want to miss the couples' dance coming up next. Go find your beau. Handsome Ted."

You mean Darcy. "Understand me first. Where I come from, we respect boundaries. We keep out of each other's . . .territories."

Helen laughed. "I don't believe that for a second. But honey, we were just passing the time till you came along. I got my marching orders a few weeks back, so no worries."

Melie ran out of the restroom, and holding up her long skirt, did her best sashay across the dance floor, flinging her arms around the neck of a very surprised Ted. "Let's do it!" she said, as the music began. A polka. She did her best, well, she was a little wild, but Ted didn't seem to care when she stepped on his feet.

The clock struck twelve. Melie pushed her damp curls off her face, made for the bar and downed a last tankard of beer. She was starting to like the stuff. She sidled up to Ted, slipping her hand in his. He squeezed her hand and leaned over to bestow a kiss on her flushed cheek. They bid farewell to Helen and Sam and the good citizens of Finn Lake and made for the door.

"Don't forget your promise, Melie," Helen yelled out.

"Huh?" Ted inquired. He stopped to wrap Melie's shawl around her shoulders as a barrier against the cool September night and steadied her as they walked to the truck.

"Something between us ladies."

"How *is* my lady?" he asked, sure of her answer.

"I can't wait to get this corset off," she replied, wincing. "How did nineteenth century women stand these things?"

"Poor Melie. I think I can help with that."

Once in the cabin, he was determined to keep his promise, but his fingers failed time and again to unlock her heart. "Don't laugh, lady. You're worried about the women. How did their gents manage? You could almost forget what you came for."

"Not you, Ted," she said, batting her eyes.

"I feel like a real butterfingers," he protested. But he reapplied himself and was rewarded. Finally his nimble fingers, refusing to be deterred by the complexities of her whale bone corset, found just the right "buttons" to trigger her release.

"Ahhh. . ."

It was the best night of her life.

When they awoke Sunday morning a little headachy, Ted asked if she'd consider spending a week up at Finn Lake, taking a little vacation. She shook her head sadly. *No, back to reality.* She had a lot to straighten out at Axis Mundi, and now she had to deal with cancer too. She didn't want to drag him into all that. He'd had one girlfriend die on him. He'd had enough *tsouris* in his life. She didn't know when or if she'd see him again.

"I have a special assignment that's going to keep me very busy, Ted."

"For how long?"

"I . . .I won't be able to see you." *Am I breaking up with him???*

Ted flashed a dark look at her. He placed his hand on his heart and bowed his head. "Suit yourself, lady." Clearly crestfallen, he left her standing in the kitchen and went to check on Gladys.

"I need you, Teddy-Baby." Gladys cried, loud enough for all to hear.

Back home Sunday night, she was getting little sleep. No friends. No lover. Dead boss. Even worse new boss (who was no doubt still planning on making her his bitch). Staff with problems. The whole Axis Mundi community with problems. Sexual predators lurking in the bushes. Grievances. Neverending crises. And . . . cancer? A fiery little lump in her right breast, Dr. Tamis had said. A live coal smoldering in her chest. How was she supposed to deal with that? Melie couldn't have problems with everyone looking to her for solutions.

Melie realized something for the first time in her life: "I don't have all the answers!" A few tears fell as she clutched Furryface to her chest.

CHAPTER XI

GOING, GOING, GONE

The next workday Melie reported back to her post, with nothing to lose, everything lost. She had often thought of how she would finally, inevitably, go bananas, ga-ga, berserk.

But now she supposed the most likely outcome was this one. She decided to sit herself, fit herself into a corner of her world, the Reception area, and see what would happen next.

Arielle caught sight of her first, scrunched into the corner, and ducked into the closet near the bathroom. "Geez," she cried from inside, "no more paper bags!"

The phones started peeping like a bunch of hungry baby birds and Arielle stumbled blindly out of the closet toward them. Before she picked up the first, she wiped the hair out of her eyes, and dared to check on Melie. She quickly turned away.

"Human Beings, good morning, how may I help you?"

Melie watched as Arielle hit the Release button, doubtless hanging up on some poor dimwit looking for a job in a lab. This dimwit's idea of benchwork experience, Melie just knew it, was like hers had been: ogling Mrs. Papadopoulos as she slinked around eighth grade Science Lab in a pink cashmere dress. Pap would heat up a cup of coffee on the Bunsen burner, lighting a fire in the groins of her pubescent teens by insisting, "Class, you must have one of all of life's experiences. I myself believe in trying everything once. Everything!"

Benchwork at Axis Mundi was anything but sexy: long hours, often middle-of-the-night hours, spent checking up on some culture or rodent or fruit fly. On the other hand, Melie supposed it depended on your definition of sexy. If it included the roving hands of middle-aged boy wonders, you were in!

"Sorry, Melie," Arielle mumbled out of habit, careful not to make eye contact.

Minutes later, Sukie breezed in and it took five additional minutes of Arielle's miming and jumping up and down till she peered over her bifocals into the corner.

"Melie's curled up behind the fish tank," Sukie announced. Arielle nodded. Then, "Get the bag—where's the bag we use on the ones that fail the typing test? She's hyperventilating. Why haven't you given her the bag?"

"There are none!" Arielle whined, whipping her head from side to side.

"I always have a bag. You just don't know where to look. Here, go try telling Melie she's scaring the fish."

"Sukie, I'm scared." Arielle was saved by the phones, all six detonating at once.

Geena bounced in then. "Hiya, everybody. Had a good weekend? Oh, Lordy, Lordy, what's this?" She ran over and crouched down, sticking her face in Melie's.

"Hi honey. How're ya feeling? Want me to do The Dance?" Geena immediately stood up and did her rendition of "Gray Skies are Gonna to Clear Up," bouncing along happily in front of the Reception couch like a 150-pound yellow baby chick. She reserved The Dance for those times when things were really going south in Employment.

Melie watched her for a moment and then stuck her left thumb in her mouth, rubbing her belly with her right hand.

"Oh, I get it. I get it. C'mon!" Geena pulled Arielle into Sukie's office.

"The phones, the phones. . ." protested Sukie weakly.

"Fuck the phones!" answered Geena, slamming the door closed.

To which Melie responded, unheard, "Let Merry Terry get 'em!"

Melie continued to study her thumb, rediscovering an old friend, popping it back in her mouth experimentally, sucking it for comfort. Life, unleashed, went on without her careful scrutiny, encouraging moments to pile clumsily into one another or stretch out in syncopated rhythms to the tune of a song of no particular merit.

The carpet seemed to vibrate under her. She looked up to see the front door opening and Doug Milty's buffalo head advancing into the unlit room. She pushed back her sleeve: 9:10!

"Hey, where is everybody?" he growled to himself.

She thought about jumping up from her cover and acting natural, but he hadn't spotted her. She hesitated.

Babs bumped the door into his wide rear end and heedlessly banged into the room.

"What's going on?" he asked her, his crossed eyes making him look more perplexed than was possible at 9:11:45 in the morning.

Babs ad-libbed, "The girls must be brainstorming in the office over there; the situation's being handled. Not to worry."

"Situation?" He ogled her ample bosom, sniffed the air, and turned to leave. "Tell Melie to call me ASAP."

The girls tiptoed out of the office and stood by as Babs hung up her raincoat and squatted down on the floor to talk to Melie.

"Keep the light off," she ordered. "Lock the door. We're closed."

Then, "Get that phone." Babs was barking.

But they did as she asked because, for one thing, they had no other plan.

Babs tugged at Melie's thumb gently and stuck it in her own mouth. "Umm, tastes pretty good. However, young lady. . ."

Melie squinted at her in anticipation.

"Of course," Babs continued, "you can stay there as long as you like, honey. But it's more comfortable under your desk. Take it from me. So c'mon."

And Melie meekly followed Babs into her office in the back.

Dr. Tamis came in for his appointment at ten while Melie was down under.

"Send him in, Arielle," commanded Babs. "Don't worry, Mel," she added as she saw Melie start to crawl out on all fours. "You rest." Melie immediately collapsed back into her prone float position.

Dr. Tamis stepped in and looked around warily.

"You're disoriented, right? Relax, it's just me, Barbara Freedman, sitting in for Ms. Kohl today. Did you have a matter to discuss with her?"

Dr. Tamis sat himself down in the visitor chair, kicking aside Melie's outstretched left leg. "You seem to have something under the desk, Ms...?"

"Just some boxes of forms. Go on."

"Ms. Freedman, I—you look somehow familiar. You even sound familiar. You know, I never forget a pretty face."

Babs coughed significantly.

"I have been taking advantage of Ms. Kohl's expertise to inform myself about modern-day etiquette relating to the intercourse between the two genders," the doctor said.

"You're not so old, Dr. Tamis! You look no more than forty? Fifty?"

"Really? I thank you for that. What I was saying, at any rate, was that I have given this a lot of thought lately. I do not want my intentions misunderstood in the future."

"Quite. I get it. Stop right there. Sex harassment, right? Want I should give it to you straight?"

"Yes, Miss, I'd appreciate your candor."

"Are you a family man? Do you date much? When's the last time you got. . .ouch!" She leaned down to rub her foot.

"Pardon?" Dr. Tamis rose halfway out of his seat.

". . .involved with someone else?"

"Oh." He sat down again. "My wife, Dr. U. Quant Tamis is, of course, quite busy working on clinical trials of Teratofloxicen."

"That tree in South America, right? See, I read the Axis Mundi Medical Center science briefs too. So you've been kinda lonely?"

"Not at all. Not at all. I've still got Lu and that new Hispanic biller looks real ripe . . ." Dr. Tamis stopped dead in his tracks. *Has he perhaps glimpsed a movement under the desk?*

"Oy." Babs quickly came around the desk and plopped herself on Tamis' lap. "Oh, Dr. T. I've been lonely too!" She nuzzled her face into the area of scraggly neck poking above his white unbuttoned labcoat. "Everybody knows you do Lucille on the exam table at four-thirty Tuesdays and Fridays, but are you otherwise available? Any other slots open?"

"Wait a minute, just wait!" He pulled back abruptly, dumping his human parcel on the floor.

Melie stuck out her legs and locked them tightly around Babs's waist, effectively immobilizing her.

Dr. Tamis didn't notice. He was staring hard at a corner of the ceiling. "Wait, you're Babs. Yes. Didn't you used to be the cardiothoracic general secretary?"

"Sort of."

"Pardon? Wait—you're out on disability, I heard. Decompensating in front of patients due to excessive strangulation by Dr. Needles? A likely story!"

"Dr. Tamis, let me tell Ms. Kohl you stopped by."

"Yes, you'd better." He left only to reenter. "If you tell anyone about this," he squeezed her prominent glands, "I'll tell them you're keeping something under your desk."

"How much you bet he didn't mean a tape recorder?" asked Melie gleefully, backing out from under the desk, waving a microcassette in the air triumphantly.

"Sit down, Mel. You look a little . . . loopy."

Melie spent most of the day napping under her desk. She, like Babs, knew a good thing when she saw it.

Later, riding home on the train, Melie fretted. What to do with Babs? Her disability leave would end in a few weeks. She couldn't send her back to that madwoman. But she had little control over the academics. It took a year or more to remove a doctor. And she'd have to sit with Merry Terry—no, she was dead—with Doug to go over all the evidence and present it to the Legal Department. She should probably give the tape to him.

She couldn't face it. She was done for. Someone else would have to continue investigating the Tamis grievance, calling in witnesses. He still didn't have a clue how to behave.

Melie was so tired of listening to herself. She started fantasizing about pulling a giant tape recorder out of her bottom drawer and setting it on the desk between her and the supplicant of the moment—take, for example, a befuddled supervisor.

There would be ten buttons, labeled as follows:

- LOW PRODUCTIVITY
- DEFICIENT PERSONALITY
- INAPPROPRIATE BEHAVIOR
- TIME THEFT
- INSUBORDINATION
- SIMPLE THEFT
- DISCRIMINATION
- WORKING WHILE UNDER THE INFLUENCE
- STATIONERY/STAPLER/STAMP THEFT
- ILLEGAL AND/OR IMMORAL ACTIVITIES

She would turn to the untrained, unwashed, unimaginative supes before her and have them identify the problem. They'd push the button together. First up would come the definition.

So TIME THEFT:

Absence, lateness, on-the-job ditziness/frequent periods of staring into space, long lunches, excessive socializing, personal phone calls, smoking pot in the stairwell.

If that fit the bill, she could then pop in cassette #2 which would direct the supe to:

SIT DOWN WITH PERPETRATOR/EMPLOYEE.
SHOW AND TELL. QUANTIFY. PRESENT PROBLEM.
SOLVE TOGETHER. SET LIMITS. STICK TO LIMITS.
DOCUMENTDOCUMENTDOCUMENT. CONSULT
HR AND EMPLOYEE ASSISTANCE PROGRAM.
FOLLOWUP WITH CONSEQUENCES. ORAL
WARNING. WRITTEN WARNING. OFF WITH
THEIR HEADS!

You know, what I do, it's not rocket science. Why can't they just take the tape with them and leave me out of it? Ah, Merry Terry would never have let this happen. Milty? Forget about it. Face it, I'm sentenced to impersonating a tape recorder for the foreseeable future. Screwed, all because I never bothered to finish that last college semester! Are they going to bury me with my boots on too?

She shuddered. She felt as though she was going to hyperventilate again. Why don't they let you open windows on these trains? she wondered. She looked around her. Her fellow commuters. She had never been one of them. Lucky ones, paired off by high school prom night, flashing their credentials just to blind her. "Look, I'm pinned!" Melie wanted to pin them with a donkey's tail.

All the times a boy took her number and never called! Her parents teased and tormented her for weeks. Why were they happy about it? Wasn't she their little princess for whom they wished all the happiness life had to offer?

Dumb supposition. You had no parents, a therapist once told her.

She didn't expect much after that. But every now and then, she had to wonder. Why can't I have something more? What's so wrong with me, anyway?

She gazed wistfully at the Ponytail Man, sitting a couple of rows in front of her and noticed he had a tiny ink stain on his shirt pocket that would surely drive him insane if he knew about it. He'd probably pull the emergency brake, hop onto the tracks, tear open his English shirt to reveal a tanned and sweet-smelling torso, stretch out his muscled arms, and wait for the oncoming train to mow right through him.

Melie must have chuckled. For he glanced up suddenly, caught her eyes. Panicked and wobbly, she stood up at the next stop and rushed out the open doors. The train doors closed and it rumbled away. Now where the hell was she?

Home later than usual, she fed the cat and headed straight to bed, hoping for a deep dream-free sleep. No such luck.

> It was her first day back at work after vacation. A clerkish man out of Kafka was sitting in her office in a newly-partitioned area by the window, back to her, bent over, eating his lunch out of a paper bag.

Some women had hung their bras and panties out to dry, using her bulletin board and all her red and green tacks. No one was in the outer office to welcome her back. Finally, Merry Terry charged in to announce that Sukie was going to be out for the day.

Melie gasped. "I can't believe she's doing this to me!"

Geena pranced in, swinging her mane of golden curls, and oblivious, asked, "So how was it?"

Melie woke up in a sweat, and her first thought was: Where was Babs in this dream? Where were all the people who needed her?

Melie decided she could best adjust to the new Doug Milty regime by learning more about her habitat, seeing it with new eyes, probably fish eyes. On her arrival at work the next morning, she perched on the edge of the black vinyl couch, with her back to a bag lady/potentially BFOQ (bona fide occupationally qualified) job candidate (God help us) to scrutinize the behavior of the denizens of the Employment Office fish tank. She diagrammed the aimless meanderings from one side of the tank to the other, top to bottom, bottom to top of Ezra, Young, and Piffy, the three resident mascot gouramis of Axis Mundi. *Aren't they the ultimate survivors, barely registering the changes in their environment?* After a while she thought, by George, she'd got it. But to be sure, she decided to continue observation throughout the day and apply her new-found knowledge that night at Grand Central Station.

To navigate through these waters, that was the idea, but also emerge unscathed of body, unbroken of spirit. To escape being swept up into a maelstrom and sucked down forever to Davy Jones's locker. To foresee the bends required, the slippery sidesteps, the mild buckling of the knees, the appropriate angle of sway to the hips, and prepare for the alternative of flattening oneself to a walking eel posture or puffing up and out like an adder, to clear a waterway of one's own.

By five PM, Piffy was, sadly, stuck sideways in a green plastic shrub up near the top of the tank and had to be counted out. Melie worried he had succumbed to the unexpected attention, the stress of performing

128

flawlessly for a very critical observer. Luckily, Ez and Young seemed to swing through their routines without a hitch. They might brush with death, she thought, but never with each other. Her idols.

Babs handled the run-of-the-mill grievants; Doug didn't have the sense to follow up on the major crises; Melie had a nice rest. Her staff knew their jobs and mostly averted their eyes and pretended she wasn't there when their attempts at prying her off the couch failed.

She retreated to her office with her notes. She was feeling so much better today! She would transcribe her notes onto a child-size yellow pad. That way she could refer to them more easily when out on the main concourse for her trial channel crossing. For she'd realized that to survive in these times, she would need to navigate locomotive as well as corporate milieus.

Leaving the office at five, she passed a couple of the detectives in the hallway between the Employment Office and the rest of HR. They were still hanging around, doing God-knows-what. None of their findings had been made public. The yellow tape had finally disappeared from Merry Terry's office doors which presumably led into the murder scene. *Why don't they just pack up and leave already? I'll feel much better when they're gone.*

Lucille materialized just then in the hallway as Melie was heading for the stairs. She wagged her finger at Melie. "Bad girl!" she said. "You're the bad girl." The detectives looked at Melie for the first time with some curiosity. Melie hightailed it down the stairs.

She hit Grand Central Station at its stormiest—six PM on a Friday evening. It was exactly ten months to the day after her fatal crossing and eventual meeting up with Mr. Dreadlock and the 350-pound conductor and the missed aisle seat and the only available perch, a middle seat between two gentlemen whose pores belched out smoke with every bump of the rail.

"I'm treading water, that's good, yeah," Melie jabbered to herself.

She had been holding her own for the last ten minutes or so, though strong undertows sometimes caused her to drift downstream toward the street or in a westerly direction toward the avenue. Quick thinking and clever sidesteps had corrected any serious deviations. She was determined to cross the main concourse with dignity and aplomb instead of scurrying around the edges as she'd been doing lately.

Thus far she had successfully steered clear of the whirlpool eddying around the Info Desk. To get into that circuit surely meant going into Info Desk Orbit nearly forever or certainly until the station closed its lights at one-thirty AM, helpless to extract one's person on one's own, alive and palpating still, but incapable of independent action, of veering off in a novel direction on a course of one's own and of one's own choosing.

Melie's feet throbbed with the tenseness of the dance. Bells rang in her ears, and the fog at the edges of things moved in to the center of her vision. She must have swayed sideways into the tall man collecting train timetables from the trays on top of the Info Desk.

"Watch it, will ya!" he shouted.

Dizzily, she peered up at him. "Oh, hi. You're the Ponytail Man," she declared brightly.

"Look, miss, I'm not asking for your comments about my hairstyle. Keep your distance is all."

He didn't remember her. "No, but I liked you," said Melie earnestly, tugging on his sleeve. "I mean, your hair, I liked."

He threw Melie a disdainful, searing look. "Look, you Fascho Single Weirdo Dyke!" He jabbed with the manicured nail on the index finger of his right hand to the thick gold band wrapped around his left ring finger. He moved off to his left, sneering.

"Dyke!" he intoned once more for good measure.

Melie closed her eyes tightly and tried to remember her mantra. *Wait, what mantra?* She opened them and felt confused. "Ezra. Piffy. Young?" she muttered. "Good. Now where was I? What have I learned from the fish?"

She saw PTM looking back at her from the doors leading to 42nd Street.

"I'll have to look you up in the DMZ!" she shouted. She realized that was not quite right, what she meant to say, and leaned back against a wall to rest, except there was no wall. Instead, she slipped into the dreaded vortex of the Info Desk. Soon tangled in designer boots and Armani pants legs, she fell flat on her ass, arms flailing like a baby octopus.

Scrambling frantically, she regained her footing—*whew!*—only to be swept into circling the Desk with the other Grand Central Station floaters. The worst of it was walking backwards, powerless to stop. She watched helplessly as the Avenue, the Street, the steps leading to the underground rail, the food court, and the ramp to the Bar, all retreated into the distance, only to reappear on the next lap around, still too far to touch or to reach.

"Will this day never end?" she demanded aloud in a torn and scratchy voice.

"Nope," answered a decrepit-looking gent in a dirty white jacket, walking backwards right in front of her.

"Dr. Tamis ?"

No response. Come to think of it, and Melie did just that, he did live on Sutton Place.

"George?"

She stopped in her tracks and he piled into her. She again landed on her rear end but this time managed to crawl out of the Info Desk vortex. Scrambling to her feet, she raced off to the gate in time to catch the late train.

Had she conquered her environment? She had no measurements, no data, no sense of it all. *All I can say is I'm a survivor.*

On Monday, worrying about Tamis' snub—did it have to do with her investigation, Babs's fumbling attempts at counseling, Melie's own status as his (doomed?) patient?—Melie arrived at her office to find someone behind her desk, in her chair with the torn vinyl seat, sipping coffee from her Axis Mundi Medical Center coffee mug.

"Good morning. You're in earlier than usual."

"What?"

"Don't worry, Mel. Why don't you take a seat over there? But perhaps you'd like to hang up your coat first on one of the hooks in Reception?"

Melie dropped her canvas bag on the floor and remained standing. She picked up subtle changes in the temperature of the room. Her professional journals, usually carefully stacked on the credenza in the corner, had the look of having been recently rifled through. Staples, scotch tape, rolodex, in-box, pencil and pen jar, tissues, telephone had all found new resting places on her desk. Finally she walked around the desk, rolled her chair with Babs in it off to the side, and peered into the wastepaper basket.

"Really?" She straightened back up.

Her weekly calendar holding all her planning, upcoming meetings, empty blocks of time to accommodate crises, and even Crises, plus a few sniveling Exits, her own weekly "Week at a Glance," was poking its curious head out of the garbage, as if to ask, "What have I done?"

Melie stood off to one side of Babs, squinting at her, then sat down in a visitor's chair. She stared at the place her calendar usually occupied and noticed a new black blotter.

"Could you get me some coffee, Babs?" she croaked. She consoled herself with the thought that at least there was no underwear pinned to her bulletin board.

When she'd had her coffee, she started giving Babs the Story: her surprise visit; attack on Gladys the parrot; the tender letter from Ted. Who else could she talk to? At a particularly telling moment in the story ("I tried to kill his animal! What's wrong with me?"), Babs reached for the tissue box on the window ledge, "Here, use as many as you like. I can always buy more. Have a good cry. There, there, it'll seem better in the morning."

After ten minutes Melie walked to the door and delivered her parting words. "It is morning! And Babs, you can do better than that. Tune in to Dr. Ruth. Study the shrink in *Unmarried Woman*. You think this is easy? Think again!"

"Going home," she told Arielle, and grabbed her coat off the hook and slammed the Reception door as hard as she could, startling the job applicants. *Hope they pee their pants!*

She'd once told a therapist—yes, she'd had one once for a few sessions—that the hardest part about her job was that she couldn't make any mistakes. People's lives depended on her! She had to make the right decision. Or people would lose their jobs, their kids would turn to teenage prostitution, crack pipes and sniffing glue, they would subsist on a diet of Hostess Twinkies and Fanta, get morbidly obese, hang out in train stations terrifying commuters. Doctors would get away with what they did without Melie to defend the employees, rescue them, fix them. . .

On the early afternoon train Melie mulled over recent happenings: *I could lose my life. Like Merry Terry. Not exactly, but still . . .*

The dream that night was so transparent:

> She'd fallen down a deep hole just walking along the sidewalk. There was no warning. No one around to help her. She was all alone. She had to get out! Who could help her?

CHAPTER XII

DISAPPEARING ACT

They were going to get her at last. Who? Why, the goons of the military-industrial complex she had been warned about so many years before—by WBAI, or was it *Laugh-In?*

She saw the events of the last few weeks building inexorably to this climax; she saw today as merely the culmination of an elaborately contrived plot, an accretion of disaster upon disaster like the layers upon layers of wallpaper she had tried to scrape off the walls of her pre-war apartment when she moved in. (Finally she had given up and added her own beige textured layer, one that had popped away from the wall in recent days.)

Each event, each mini-crisis had seemed nothing out of the ordinary, another full moon sung to the tune of "Blue Moon," another bad day at Black Rock. One more transfer candidate on the edge of the ledge, one more exasperated doctor-supervisor, one more administrator in over her inexperienced head, one more hebephrenic giggling in Reception or unsuspecting registrar waiting to be walked over to the inpatient psych ward. One more illogical request from a department chairman, one more human rights commission questionnaire, one more joke, one more verbal bludgeoning by Merry Terry or more macho posturing by Doug, one more cosmic joke.

But like the wallpaper coming unglued after years of staying in place . . . .It was a crisis, that's what she thought. And she certainly knew how to handle crises—that was her job. Was her job. Was her job.

On this her last day at Axis Mundi Medical Center, she strode past Reception straight into her office and plopped her bag down on her desk. "Babs, get out of my chair!"

"Oh, Mel. I just put on a new coat of polyurethane . . ."

"What?"

"My nails, look." She waved short stubby fingers tipped with globs of metallic red.

"I like Amazon Red myself."

"Oh no—too blatant. Never get you anywhere, Mel. No good." Babs shook her head from side to side.

Melie frowned. "I'm going out now," Melie said as she picked up her bag. She'd lost her place. Literally.

"Have a good walk. And can you pick me up a coffee, very light with three sugars, on your way back? And two slices with everything on it. Anchovies too."

"Junk Food Imperialist!"

"Pardon?"

Melie shook her head and turned to leave.

"Will ya?"

"Yes!" she bellowed. "Everything on it," she repeated on her way out.

Arielle looked up and then down quickly. Sukie and Geena came out of their offices to stare.

Sukie called out, "Bring back some chocolate, that's a dear."

Geena gave her the once over. "Oh, boss, I like your ... er ... skirt."

"I've had this one since sixth grade, you know," Melie bragged.

"Yes, I can see that." Geena smiled. "Very cute. Very cute." Geena patted Melie on the shoulder and opened the door. A gentle push got her started in the direction of the street. The last thing she heard was Geena asking, "What are we going to do with her?"

Later . . .

"Who would believe this life? Right, Babs?"

Babs had sunk into a late-morning snooze atop Melie's former desk. The intercom rang insistently, always in the same key, rather like a mantra. Melie rested her head on the visitor side of the desk.

She popped up, hearing something.

Geena was standing in the doorway looking like the huntress Diana, a massive blonde fury with blazing hair flowing behind her, feet apart, hands on her ample hips. She looked from Babs to Melie to Babs to Melie to Babs.

"No bow and arrow?" queried Melie.

"Huh?" Geena's hands dropped helplessly to her sides.

"You look like Diana . . . oh never mind. Whatyahuntin?"

Geena shook her head sadly, turned to leave, then came back in. "Snap out of it, Ms. Kohl. Will you please!"

As soon as she left, Sukie marched in. "Babs, get up. Go get a cup of coffee from the guy downstairs."

Babs rubbed her eyes and stretched like the fat Persian cat she was. Finally she nodded agreeably and ambled out.

"Quick, Mel, get in your chair!"

Melie ducked under the desk and emerged in her rightful chair, just as Babs reentered, looking startled and displeased.

"Do you have an appointment?" demanded Sukie who was barring her way.

"No, of course not."

"Call back after four PM and close the door on your way out. We're having a private conversation here."

Surprisingly, Babs exited.

With just Sukie and herself in the room, Melie felt the room to be nevertheless overcrowded, the air crackling like high tension wires.

"I made you an appointment with my hairdresser at noon, the manicure place at one-thirty and Doug Milty at four. Got it?"

"Yes. But why?"

"Just do it."

"But what should I say to him? I mean, I could tell him I want my job back, but do I? Honestly?"

Sukie came over and took Melie's face in her hands. She spoke slowly, enunciating each word. "Melie, you still have your job. Yes, you want to keep it. You just need to bring him up to date on the work you've been handling. The crises, you know."

Melie shook Sukie off. "But why?"

Sukie picked up the intercom. Geena soon came in and stood behind her and Arielle joined them too. "Because we want you. Axis Mundi needs you."

"Oh. That." Melie looked out the window at the falling snow. *Where were they last night when I fell down that hole?*

Geena added, "Tell the hairdresser you want it bobbed in back and longer on the sides."

Melie passed the detectives on her way out. Why couldn't they zero in on someone else? Doug Milty—what was his alibi? How did they know he didn't do it? They were always planting themselves in Reception or Benefits or talking and flirting with Lucille, Lord knows why. Lucille even went out for drinks with them, some said.

Melie wished they would just go. Who really cared? Maybe those files fell down by themselves? Was Merry Terry's family pushing this investigation? Hardly. Her hubby had been swept up into a facility for people with diminished capabilities. Or so she'd heard.

She wondered what went on in a place like that.

At four PM, after the manicure and haircut, Melie headed over to D building to ask Doug Milty about her job, but when she got to his office, she hesitated in front of the closed door. Should she knock or just walk in? Dilemma. Did she want to signal Power or Obedience to Authority? *How do I know what price he will exact for granting my wishes?* His door needed repainting.

She bent down to see if there was any light under the door. She thought she could see two pairs of feet in there, one wearing high heels. Those ankles looked familiar! It was very quiet though.

She straightened up as Doug's secretary, Annabelle, walked in from lunch, clutching her coat, newspaper, hat, gloves, coffee.

"Mel?" she ventured. "What are you doing here?" She appeared frightened.

Melie shrugged. "Do you know your Styrofoam cup of coffee sludge is leaking?"

Annabelle grimaced, her cashmere beige gloves with the tips of fingers one and three now brown and wet. She smiled crookedly at Melie. "I like those hoop earrings on you? Going for a different look, are you?"

Melie touched her ears. "Just got them at the hairdresser's."

"Melie, are you okay?"

"Why not?" Melie asked cautiously, then repeated, "Not."

"Oh."

Melie stood very still. She tried to decipher the voices whispering behind the door. Was that Babs? Was Babs a turncoat? After all Melie had done for her? Rescued her from Dr. Needles, given her a safe haven under her desk, listened to her sad tales of evenings spent around the little round table in her kitchen, under a bare light bulb, with her semi-demented mother, the stresses of dating a sanitation worker—and his brother. Could Babs have been turned, after the long sessions of sharing and caring in Melie's office these last few months? It was a perjury not to be borne, hardly to be imagined!

"Have a seat. Some weather we're having, huh?" Annabelle was trying hard.

Melie sat on Annabelle's typing chair behind Annabelle's desk, which sent Annabelle into a scurry of activity. She opened the door to Doug's office, turned on the light, started dusting his black telephone, desk blotter, the leather back of his chair. Did Melie hear an inside door close and footsteps?

Annabelle came out of the office to see what Melie was up to. Satisfied that Melie was still plunked down in the same place, she went back into the inside office and yelled, "I have to make a call now." Melie could hear her mumbling something quickly into the mouthpiece and hanging up.

Melie felt an urgency overcome her. She jumped up, yelling, "Drop dead!" and quickly decamped.

As she ran out of the building, Annabelle yelled after her, "Why'd you say that to me, Mel?"

"You know!" said Melie. "And by the way, Annabelle, where were you that day Milty pulled out his Johnson and waved it at me? I could have used an ally that day."

"Sick day?" Annabelle mumbled.

"Right." Melie had a sudden urge to talk to Lucille. Before the white coats came. About a leave. One sentence from her favorite book kept running through her head: *Just because you're paranoid doesn't mean they're not after you.*

139

"See ya." Melie waved to Annabelle who ran back inside the office to her ringing telephone. Melie heard her locking the outer door.

Lucille processed the short-term disability paperwork silently as Melie stood over her. Melie refused to sit, not wanting to appear any smaller than she already was. When Lucille asked if it were a physical or mental disability, Melie just gave her a look. "Isn't it all the same thing finally?"

Melie could see Lucille didn't like that answer so she produced a note from Dr. Tamis that she had been holding onto all week about the breast cancer, the treatment, blahblahblah. "You can go now," Lucille advised. "You have twelve weeks disability leave, which means we hold the job till December 27th. You can always come in for the Christmas party." Then she whispered, "I'd advise you never to come back."

"That's a strange thing for you to say. Isn't it?" Melie commented. "I guess I'll go collect my stuff."

"No, Melie," Lucille said sternly, standing up. "Leave now and we'll ship your things to you. That's standard operating procedure, as you know."

"Nice to be treated with dignity. No ten-year pin?"

"Get out!" snarled Lucille.

On her way out, Melie noted the two security men standing around in the outer office. "Now you show up!" she yelled.

Oh, what the hell, thought Melie, suddenly very tired. She made sure to slam the door on her way out. She paused and was pretty sure she could hear them rejoicing on the other side of the door.

"I give up. They got me. What else is there to say?"

Contrary to Lucille's instructions, Melie made her way back to the Employment office. No way was she leaving without bidding farewell to her staff and collecting her favorite Head Honcho coffee mug, her edge-of-the-ledge poster, and her dream journal. In passing Arielle at the Reception desk, she noted her unusual pallor and wondered what had been going on while she was out. She stuck her head into Sukie's office, interrupting her interview with a research technician, but was confounded by Sukie's elaborate hand signals and mouthings. Geena popped out of her office too, held a finger to her lips, and gestured towards Melie's office in the back.

"Great haircut!" Geena said aloud, then covered her mouth and shooed Melie away.

Primed for an ambush of some kind, Melie walked into her office. Doug Milty was sitting in her chair and Dr. Tamis was stationed by the window, no doubt watching the young interns stroll by.

Now what? she wondered. *Hasn't Milty touched base with Lucille? Or Annabelle? What's Tamis doing here?"*

Dr. Tamis began speaking without giving her a chance to sit down. "It has come to our attention—"

"George, as her immediate supervisor, better let me," interrupted Milty.

Dr. Tamis shook his head in agreement. Melie kept her focus on Tamis, wrinkling her brow.

"Melie," continued Milty, "Dr. Tamis is here at my request."

Oh, will these clowns get on with it?

Milty stood up and began. "Ms. Kohl, since I took over the department of human resources upon the death of Terry K. Quincent, I have asked you to complete several assignments. I told you that Lucille in records needed to be put out to pasture for her histrionics. That was something like nine months ago. Back in my home state of Pennsylvania, we call that insubordination. Further investigation into your record these last months has revealed that you allowed your staff the Monday after Dean Terry's passing to leave the phone unmanned. At such a crucial and critical time for the medical center, the very moment employees, temps, interns and vendors needed to be reassured that life at Axis Mundi Medical Center would go on as usual, you shirked your duty." He wagged his finger in her direction. And popped a button.

Melie made her way to the visitor chair and demurely sat down, barely suppressing a smile. "And you, Dr. Tamis, what is it you'd like to accuse me of?"

Dr. Tamis coughed once, wiped his mouth with an embroidered hanky, possibly a sucking-up present from Sukie at some point in the past, and said, "Melie—Ms. Kohl, you have dragged my good name through the mud with your incessant probings and investigations into what a girl with a tenth grade education, Keisha Anne Woods, has told you. She has no credibility here, yet you persevered. Keisha Anne Woods herself has told me that she feels you ignored her—"

"Isn't that a contradiction?" Melie broke in, looking from one to the other.

"Look," said Milty, "we don't get involved in these cases much. The Dean always left it up to Terry to resolve these piddling claims. Now we got you messing everything up."

"So what's going to happen now, guys?" Melie asked as she grabbed her mug off a shelf, accidentally dislodging her copy of <u>Best Practices in Employment Law 1990</u> which fell to the floor with a splat. As she picked it up and put it back on the shelf, she flashed the cover at them and winked. Then she made her way around her desk, and pushed Milty's belly back a tad, opening the desk drawer to retrieve her journal. "I've got somewhere to be. So can we speed this up?"

"There is also the matter of Barbara Freedman, known commonly as Babs, who has been allowed to circulate freely throughout the medical center, taking on all sorts of responsibilities, although she is widely regarded as unstable," continued Milty.

"Unstable because Dr. Needles has been choking her on and off for most of this year, and you, Doug, have done squat to remedy the situation. That lawsuit should be coming to your desks sometime soon."

Milty blanched. "I knew nothing about it," he protested.

"Exactly." Melie bobbed her head up and down gleefully. She hadn't told him a thing.

Dr. Tamis and Doug Milty eyed each other nervously. Milty banged his fist on the desk and pointed at her. "As your supervisor, I am forced to terminate you effective immediately for insubordination and deficient job performance."

"I see." Melie felt incipient hysteria rising in her throat, but beat it back with great effort. She closed her eyes, silently recited the opening stanzas of *La Marseillaise,* then opened them. "May I speak now? Listen up, gents. Here's my five minute refresher course in employment law. Number one: I am a female over the age of 40, thus a minority protected by Age Discrimination legislation. Two: I am by definition now considered disabled—did you forget, Dr. Tamis? I am covered by the Americans with

Disabilities Act. Three: I have ten years' tenure at Axis Mundi during which my performance appraisals have all been satisfactory or better. You'll be hard pressed to find a warning of any type in my HR file, and progressive discipline is the name of the game when it comes to wielding the axe." Melie was just warming up now. "Don't forget for a minute how many times I have represented the center at the Human Rights Commission hearings on 125th Street. Or been deposed in employee lawsuits. Or conducted investigations into grievances by our staff. Do you gentlemen realize I have never lost a case for the center? Maybe you should have a chat with our legal counsel before you pepper me with your allegations."

Doug Milty was sweating profusely and trying in vain to loosen his florid tie. Dr. Tamis looked at Milty angrily as if to say: Why didn't we know all this beforehand? He crumbled up the script Doug had been reading from and gestured to Melie to get out.

Melie glanced at her watch. "Oh dear, I really must be going. Now that Lucille's approved my disability leave for the next twelve weeks, I must get started taking care of myself." She stood up, dusted herself off, gathered her few possessions, and walked out of the office, closing the door ever so quietly.

A quick hug to her startled staff and a nod to the sprinkling of candidates who were gathered outside her door trying to eavesdrop, and Melie was on her way.

The message light on her phone was blinking when she got home. The first message was from Dr. Tamis' office: "Ms. Kohl, your surgery is scheduled for Friday at three. Follow the directions on the printout we gave you."

Then: "Melie, hi there. I wanted to tell you something. I think you made a good impression on Helen. She doesn't like many people but she likes you. Things are status quo up here. Weather is getting pretty cold and we still have six inches of snow on the ground from the storm last week—"

Melie erased the messages and tried to erase the sound of Ted's voice and the memory of his strong arms encircling her waist. She fed and watered Furryface, undressed, and put herself to bed without any supper.

CHAPTER XIII

NOW WHAT? CALLING THE LONE RANGER!

Now Melie had to take care of herself and the little bitty lump of malignant cells lodged in her right breast. Tamis had suggested a lumpectomy since the cancer was in the very early stages. True he was a womanizer and a slug, but his reputation as a doctor was impeccable. She'd asked Sukie to research other options for her—there was some disagreement in the medical community about whether such an operation was even necessary for this type of cancer—but the conclusion was *Cut it out*.

So he did.

In the weeks following the procedure, Melie made a concerted effort to let go. For ten years she'd been wallowing in people up to her neck. They'd almost pulled her under. Her brain had been on overdrive: *find a solution, find a solution, find a solution!* She'd had no time nor energy to keep herself from drowning.

Now she slept late; she unearthed a cookbook; she tried to teach herself to knit. Still, fixing herself some meager meals, picking up some dropped stitches, and watching the daytime soaps left her with too much time on her hands. She brooded over missed opportunities and felt her sanity getting even more slippery on her. At least once a day she caught herself rehearsing whole conversations in her living room with invisible denizens of Axis Mundi. *Take that, Milty!*

She tried to focus on the rest of her life. Disability payments would run out in three months' time. Fortunately, she was on paid leave due to all the sick time she'd accrued. Nevertheless, what was she to do? Go back to Axis Mundi? She couldn't face that. She'd blown a gasket somewhere in her head or heart. No longer could she play the Answer Lady, Go-To Person or Ms. Fix-it. Could she get another job?

How about working in a shoe store? She didn't care much about shoes. One plus. There could hardly be many complaints and certainly no investigations into bad behavior. Soon she'd be well enough, maybe next week, to canvas local stores to see if they needed a saleswoman. She needed something local. Forget about commuting to the city: the grimy train windows, the strung-out commuters, the crowds threatening to spill over onto the tracks.

She had passed the psych consult Dr. Tamis had insisted on. Easy peasy—she knew all the right answers. *Don't ever cop to hearing voices. Or uncontrollable anger. Or paranoid delusions.* She'd been clever enough to keep all hallucinations, waking dreams, dream dreams, and unorthodox coping mechanisms to herself.

They were expecting her back at the end of December. Her staff. Axis Mundi Medical Center. Who knew what messes they were concocting without her even hand? The thing of it was—she needed the money and the medical benefits. She supposed that shoe stores might provide some coverage. And she might even make more money if she got a job that gave her commissions plus a salary. But she was forgetting something. What if she was turned down because of her preexisting conditions? She paced the small living room, back and forth in front of the television, searching for solutions.

One rainy day, she stopped her pacing to put the TV on. Time for the soaps.

Pity I don't have their beauty, their youthful exuberance, their malevolence. Nor their gorgeous hunks of manhood with outstretched arms to catch me when I fall.

She thought briefly of Ted's arms, the furry softness of them, his strength when he lifted her off her feet for an embrace. "That's over," she reminded herself. "He won't want me now."

She turned up the volume. She didn't want to miss any of the story she had been following these last weeks. Would Simon's mother reveal the truth about his father in time for Simon to cancel his wedding to the woman who was conceivably his half-sister? Would this happen before his fiancée had surgery to make her look more like Simon's first wife? Was his mother really intending to run off with the termite exterminator, the tall blond hunk from Denmark?

The doorbell rang. Strange! She lowered the volume on the TV. It rang again.

Ted walked down the three steep steps to her door and then had to stoop to enter the apartment. He remained bent over slightly, standing in the middle of the living room, for the ceiling seemed perilously close to the top of his curly grey head.

He took everything in quickly: the shades of grey and brown, the sturdy wood furniture with straight lines and straight angles, the empty wastepaper basket, the book resting on the kitchen table next to a bowl with a single crabapple, the small windows set high in the basement walls, the faint sound of children in the back courtyard.

"Mel, this place is not you." He pulled her into her own living room, put his hands on her shoulders to face her outwards, and pointed out everything silently.

She gazed up at him, puzzled.

"But Ted, this is where I live."

"But you, you're red and orange and green and purple and blue feathers."

"You've got me confused with your damn bird!"

He just shook his head at that. He peeked into her bedroom and found the framed poster over her bed. "Ah, wait now. Here it is. A piece of Melie at last."

Melie followed him in. They studied the picture. A man and a woman cling to each other in a deserted courtyard. Late afternoon or evening. Cherubs tumble over each other and try to hide on the stone portal behind them. Trellises of tiny pale blue and pink flowers wind around them. He, in a long brown robe, embracing her tenderly, with eyes on her face alone. She, pale, looking inward, or ahead into the future, knowing more than he ever will. A single porcelain-like blue plant blooms by her side.

Ted reached behind him and pulled Melie close. He gazed down on her and gestured around her room. "Listen, Melanie Kohl. This life is not the one you want. You want what's in that picture. Except that I'm not quite that cute and boyish anymore, am I?"

She smiled faintly. "I just bought that the other day."

"How about this? I'm going to bring you out of that ruined courtyard, and you're going to do the same for me. See those thorns there? They look almost like barbed wire. It's time for little Adam and Eve to move into the light. What do you say?"

Melie broke away and headed back to the living room. She sat down at the table and began opening her mail.

"Mel," he continued, sitting down opposite her, "I used to think I couldn't ask you to give your big city life up for me. I couldn't risk it. Again, I mean."

She stopped opening her bills and met his eyes across the table. Her own eyes welled with tears. "What do you want from me?" she pleaded.

"Come live with me and be my love/And we will all the pleasures prove. . . ." He paused to scratch his head. Then he intoned:

"Come into the garden, Maud,/For the black bat, night has flown,/ Come into the garden, Maud,/I am here at the gate alone. . . ." He stopped. Melie's mouth dropped open. She looked down at her bills again. He strode over to the high window overlooking the courtyard.

"You need a tree outside your window. A deer or two. You even need fishing! You need—"

"You." Melie crept up behind him and encircled his waist with her thin arms. She rested her head on his back.

He spun around and swept her into his arms, laughing. He carried her into her room and laid her down under the telltale painting. As he undressed her, he asked softly, "Are you ready?"

"Ted, I really truly want you. Only. . . ."

His hands paused midair.

"You have to help me pack. I'm a terrible—"

He sank down upon his woman then, covering her lips with his own, matching his body to hers, degree by degree, rhythm for rhythm. They were in the blasted courtyard, but it was the day that dawned behind them now.

There she was on a swing on a hillside overlooking verdant plains far below. She recognized her own pale face and curly cropped hair but, but, the hair was milky white! Suddenly there appeared a man—was it Ted?—who stood in front of her and started to push her. She noticed with his first push that her hair was now flowing down her back. She was wearing a pinafore with ruffles and frills, and laughing, throwing her head back and laughing. . .

When she neared him and tucked her long straight legs in, he reached out and playfully gave the seat of the swing a hearty shove, saying, "Go a-way!"

She swung gracefully back, legs tucked under the swing, smiling as if she knew something he did not. The swing swung towards him again.

They played Go a-way for a long time it seemed, and she never tired of pumping her legs in and out, and he never tired of telling her to "Go away," knowing she'd be back.

It was a great game—so romantic—and when she awoke from this dream, she was still smiling. She closed her eyes and wrote an ending:

He caught her as the swing slowed and wrapped her in a bear hug. Then they walked together, arm in arm, down the hillside to a little cabin with smoke curling out of the chimney. . .

Oh—is that what Melie wants?

EPILOGUE

Something was jumping back and forth over Melie's head as she lay in bed—her twenty-five pound calico cat. When she landed after the fifth pass, Melie shoved her off the bed and fixed her with her steeliest stare. Furryface slunk away but Melie knew she'd be back.

"Is that you, City Girl?" asked Ted who she could hear bustling around in the kitchen.

If I don't answer, I'll get another few minutes . . .

"I'm making you Uncle Ted's country breakfast: stuffed French toast, Canadian bacon and lemon tart for dessert."

If I don't answer. . .

Smoky, eggy, rich aromas were making their way her way. Melie pulled the comforter over her face and managed to drift off until. . . .

"Ow! Something's nibbling on my toes," she shrieked, bounding out of bed, holding up one foot.

"Hey, that's my job." Ted said. Coming into the sleeping alcove, he shooed the cat away. He pushed Melie back on the bed and began demonstrating.

What are you doing? she thought to ask, but then again. . . *Why not enjoy it?*

Soon Ted was stroking her leg higher and higher and snaking his other arm up her torso, closer and closer to "the girls," cupping them in his straight-from-the-oven-fresh hands.

"Ted. . .Ted. . ."

"You were saying?"

An hour later Melie sat in a cane-backed bird-shredded chair drawn up close to the breakfast table, holding her breath. Through the sliding back doors, she watched the approach of the lame deer. He came to sniff at her back deck and pee on her snowed-in flower garden, lifting his head every few seconds to study the wind for danger: hunters? dogs? rain?

He seemed always to come by at this hour, as she lingered over breakfast, but never more often than once in two weeks. Melie wondered where else the deer visited, whose back decks in all of Finn Lake he chose to honor with his inspection, where he left his scent and why. She longed mostly to go with him to learn what he knew.

When he had turned back to the woods, she returned to flipping through *FindersKeepers* for new items for their home while scraping together and scooping up one last satisfying mouthful of lemon tart crumbs from the sides of the chipped white porcelain dish.

Ted had run over to a neighbor's to help move a piano. She was content to be alone with her thoughts and her animals. Gladys was up and preening, eyeing the results in her mirror. A truce had been declared: Gladys would always be welcome in their house but all bowed to Melie, the Alpha Female. Had Gladys given up her sovereignty without a backward squawk? The addition of Furryface to their household may have had something to do with Gladys' new attitude. Melie had caught Furryface, her fat lazy feline, licking her lips once or twice, and making that awful clicking sound deep in her throat, the way cats do when they're stalking prey. *Maybe we should rename her Furocious?* Gladys was no fool and kept an anxious eye on the food pantry, becoming visibly agitated any time the stores of cat food were low.

Brimming over with goodwill, Melie had already fed the bird and cleaned her cage upon awakening. Furryface had been introduced to the great outdoors; no more catbox for her. She loved the freedom to come and go. Melie realized she'd be relieved to see her bring in a mouse or two—and so would Gladys.

December, yet the day was turning out to be shiny and bright and unseasonably warm. A light breeze caressed her cheek as it blew through the open windows. For Christmas, next week, they'd be going to a dress-up party at Helen and Sam's and it sounded like fun. For Hanukkah Melie had shown Ted how to light his first menorah. As a reward she'd given him eight little presents, one of which was a brand-new sparkling clean cover for Gladys' cage.

These would be her first happy memories of the season. She was still amazed that she no longer had to sit at the HR party, clucking over some insulting gift from her boss. December from now on meant sleigh rides and snowball fights, cross-country skiing, eggnog, and snuggling with her lover in a cabin built for two. *Three if we count Gladys. Four: let's not forget the fierce and frightful Furocious Furryface ready to make Gladys toe the line if she reverts to any of her old tricks.*

Melie's time was now her own. No desk calendar ruled her days. No medical personnel staging ambushes. She could choose how to spend her time: helping Ted out in the Shoppe, reconfiguring the displays or dealing with suppliers or just dusting and tidying up; helping women to select the most flattering blouse or decide which authentic grandfather clock to set in their foyer; helping men appreciate the female perspective when it came to purchasing a brooch or a pair of earrings for their wives; helping the children get the most pleasure from the simple toys of yesteryear.

In her free time—well, all her time was free—she intended to work at becoming part of the community. Ted's idea. She'd already volunteered at the library whenever an extra pair of hands was needed, and in a few weeks she was slated to start tutoring a young boy from Bosnia in English as a second language.

Melie's blessings were palpable and real, yet she struggled this morning to put a finger on her rising discontent. *What's wrong?* Hadn't she everything she'd always wanted? A man of her own, sexy and smart, who gave her back as good as she gave and would always be a challenge to understand and to love. A strangely welcoming stepdaughter, and a stepson, still to meet. A comfortable abode—a home— in rustic surroundings with quaint and crumbling artifacts, like that beautiful old loom in the corner with its half-finished carpet strung across it, that she'd unearthed in the Shoppe— much better than ordinary furniture and décor. The Pre-Raphaelite poster held center stage on the wall behind the settee. She felt the first stirrings of friendship with some of the locals, yes, even Helen Call, generally acknowledged to be the town gossip. They had a lot in common—both needed to know everything about everyone, albeit for different reasons. Oh, they had Ted in common too. She knew that. But everyone had a past, didn't they?

And how could she forget? Nothing in her lymph nodes. No further treatment needed at the moment. Dr. Tamis said she would be fine! *He also said, Begone, foul wench!*

Melie told herself over and over she had escaped a dark barren basement of a life. For God's sake! She was in a far far better place.

A place—maybe that's what was missing, she thought, rising to fetch a fresh mug of First Avenue brew. Aimlessly, she started to pace the room.

What is my place in all this? she asked herself. *I'm a companion, lover, co-shopkeeper if need be, brooding fisherwoman and nagging fishwife by turns.*

Now she was on to something.

Suddenly she stopped dead in her tracks and flung open the front door for she had a craving, a giant physical calling to be at Axis Mundi Medical Center in New York City right at that very moment in time. The wind blew right through her; her fingers and toes tingled.

When Ted returned just after ten, Melie announced, "Ted, I'm thinking of taking a little trip."

Ted brought another slice of lemon tart to the table, watching Melie out of the corner of his eye. "Not a lot of cars passing."

"None."

"Not a lot of action. . ."

"Oh, Ted," she said, shaking her head, "just let it go."

"Right."

"Who's my Teddy Baer?" She leaned over the table, giving him a peck on the lips, and waited.

He threw down his fork, stood and sent his chair flying, and administered an 8.5 Richter scale grizzly bear hug and kiss.

"You take my breath away," she whispered. "But I must get ready." With a coquettish wink, she disappeared into the sleeping alcove to dress. "There's a train in fifteen minutes."

"Get a move on, girl," Ted called out to her. "I may be going to Walter's for a while to see if we can finish sanding those bookshelves. Meet you here to "cook" a three-bean salad at about five?"

"Sukie, you look the same. No one would ever guess you're seventy-five—such skin, such a glow." Melie sat in her old office, in the visitor chair, noting the pink and blue stuffed bears on the windowsill, the cheery motivational calendar urging the kitten to just "hang in there."

"How are you managing, Suke?"

"Oh, Mel, I miss you! Remember what you always said about me? I thrive on disaster."

"Yes, a good thing. So tell me everything, slowly. No fast. Oh, it's so good to see you. Though this place is more depressing and dingy that I can believe. I just never realized." She took in the light green walls, the government issue metal desk, the windows sticky with New York City grit.

"Mel, after your . . . sudden decision to leave. . ."

"Breakdown!"

"No . . . . You had a physical problem."

"Whatever." Seeing Sukie's expression, she added, "Right. That was the easy part. The lumpectomy. The right breast. And they got it all."

"Thank God. So—Babs lasted a couple of weeks more. I mean, the crises were piling up outside our door. We needed the extra help. Finally Tamis told Milty who she really was and she was persuaded—correction: she 'volunteered'—to accept a new job as registrar in dermatology."

"But that's a lower position."

"Have you forgotten how things work at Axis Mundi or rather how people's minds work here? Think. What's the appeal of derm to someone like Babs?"

"You mean . . . ?"

"Botox and—"

"Lipo!"

"She'll get along great with DeeDee," said Melie. "Both like to color outside the lines."

"And I think she's—how do you say that?—'boffing' the two of them!" Sukie laughed as she said this, shaking her head, wide-eyed.

"Milty and Tamis? More power to her! I mean, 'Yuck!'" Melie leaned back and grinned. "You really can't make this stuff up, right Sukie?"

The new girl up front popped her head in to tell them they were making a little too much of a racket. So they shushed her out of the room. They decided to continue their reunion at the corner deli. Melie learned that Geena had finally had a blind date opportunity that paid off. She was getting married in the summer to a fabulously wealthy stock trader. Arielle had moved up a few notches, doing computerized patient billing in urology. (Arielle—who knew?—much preferred fighting with insurance companies to witnessing applicants taking their pants off, employees brandishing knives, or bosses turning up murdered.)

"And Dr. Needles, the strangling doc?" Melie inquired.

"Finally given the heave-ho. With a year's pay of course. and a glowing recommendation."

"Of course, of course. They might run into her at a medical convention, you know. Okay, now for the big question. Who's your Daddy, Sukie?"

"Uncle Milty, of course, dean of finance and human resources. He still hasn't got a clue. He wants to cut back on all the benefits and thinks we're paying our people outlandishly high salaries."

"Yikes."

"But I'm bringing him around. He's learning. What goes . . ."

". . . around comes around. Oh, Suke." Melie reached out to clasp her hand.

They finished off a huge wedge of cheesecake, gulped down with three or four cups of coffee, which set Melie's fingers to trembling.

"Sukie, by the way, whatever happened with the background check project?"

"Oh please. We got bigger fish to fry. It's filed and forgotten."

Sukie stood up.

"I'm so happy for you, Mel. And I'll come out to Finn Lake—maybe in the summer and spend a weekend. Don't forget your present."

Melie took her old AMMC nameplate wrapped in old recycled Christmas paper and gave Sukie a hug.

They parted in front of the deli. Sukie hugged Melie tightly but paused to get her dainty white hanky out of her purse and wipe the tears off Melie's cheeks. "You were right to get out of this place. You have a nice quiet life now. Be happy."

Melie nodded and started to cry for real.

"Put some zing into it, girl. You're not a quiet type." Sukie winked and trotted away toward the main building of Axis Mundi Medical Center. Then she shouted, "Wait!" and came running back to Melie.

"I can't believe I forgot to tell you—Lucille was arrested last week for the murder of Merry Terry!"

"Omigod, I saw that in the paper! What was the motive? I mean, more than for any of the rest of us?"

"We should have guessed. Merry Terry had your preliminary notes on the investigation into sexual harassment charges, and you know Merry Terry, she would have pursued it to the ends of the earth."

"You mean Tamis, right?"

"Yes! I learned from Babs that Tamis had been bonking Lucille for years. Years! Everybody knew it."

"I didn't."

"Me neither. Lucille must have thought Tamis was going to get kicked out of Axis Mundi, be forced to relocate, and leave her in the lurch."

"But he's married with four kids!"

Sukie gave her a you-should-know-better-at-your-age look. "Lucille snuck in through the side door and gave Terry's file cabinet one hell of a shove."

"Geez."

"But apparently, Merry Terry was still kicking. So she bashed Merry Terry's head in with <u>Best Practices in Employment Law 1990</u>. And that didn't do it. Frantic, she grabbed Merry Terry's own HR Warrior glass award off her bookshelf and creamed her with it. You should see the pictures! That Merry Terry was one hell of a tough broad."

"Ew! How'd they figure out it was Lucille? Did someone finger her?"

"In a way. Remember the cleaning woman? Well, she was in shock after walking in on a dead dean and a passed-out CFO. She took off on a leave of absence and spent most of this year recovering at home in rural Guatemala. No phone service. The detectives gave up the idea of questioning her further. Lo and behold, she returned to Axis Mundi to work. First thing she did was to take one of the choir boys to those bathrooms downstairs—you know the ones?—where he found the bloodied murder weapon—with Merry Terry's blood and Lucille's fingerprints smeared all over it."

Sukie paused for breath. "And now for the *coup de résistance*: Lucille's in jail. For life."

At least she got out of this place!

"To think some people suspected you!" Sukie blurted out. "But I never—"

Just when I think I've heard everything . . .

Recovering her composure, Melie demanded to know, "What's Tamis doing? Did Babs play that tape we made to anyone?"

"Not hardly."

"How come?"

"Ready? It's like this. George Baedeker Tamis is the new Dean of Axis Mundi Medical Center!"

"WHAAAAT?"

"You must have heard the old Dean went back to his horse farm in Virginia? Tamis was the natural successor: such a fine specimen of a man. A preeminent scholar. And one of the world's top surgeons."

Melie just stared.

"You haven't asked about Keisha Anne Woods," said Sukie, changing tack. "She's sporting a sleek new sealskin jacket along with this incredible watch that does everything but drink your coffee for you. That girl—I never trusted her."

Walking slowly back to Grand Central Station, Melie suddenly spied Ponytail Man/PTM sitting in a café with a rather drab-looking woman. Melie hid herself behind a tree to get a better look.

That was his wife. No doubt about it. She seemed to be haranguing him about something or other, gesticulating wildly, as he feigned an exaggerated interest in his expresso and the business section of the *Wall Street Journal*. After a few minutes he risked looking at her, and his expression of unmitigated disgust was chilling. His wife seemed to catch the look and closed her eyes for a second.

Melie had seen enough. She walked on. Another fate she had narrowly escaped? Yes, and another fantasy not grounded in reality.

Back at the ranch, Melie saw there was no home but this one to go back to. She started putting more energy into searching for Sukie's "zing": she attended the gardening club, a Chinese vegetarian cooking class, tried raising rabbits and ducks. She worked a shift as hostess at Lucian's on alternate weekends. Not the kind of "zing" she craved. Then right after Christmas, she found it.

An ad in *FindersKeepers*:

WANTED: Man or Woman. Volunteer in a program for teenaged mothers, most with a history of substance or other abuse, preferably 3 PM's/wk.

Needed: illusion of serenity + strong stomach. Helps to like people.

Note: must be able to man Crisis Line during full moons.

Excellent benefits.

Within a few weeks, Melie had all the "zing" she could handle MWF afternoons and gratefully looked forward on Tuesdays and Thursdays to hours of fishing on the lake and snuggling in a rowboat with Ted. If things ever got too slow, she would meet up with Sheila in the city for a Girls' Day Out to laugh about Ted and his foibles and to chuckle over Sheila's latest blind date opportunities.

Melie now had everything she needed. Who could ask for anything more? Well, Ted had said if she wanted, he could arrange to have a little Baer running around! *Yikes!* She agreed to give it some thought, but was she good mommy material? She still felt very much like an understudy for the role of girlfriend/partner/lover. Granted, she was a fast learner—in her deepening relationship with Ted, she'd figured out which buttons to push and which to avoid. And that was world enough for her.

Here she was on a swing again, this time in a Maxfield Parrish kind of painting, colored in deep blues and pinks. Her curly brown locks flowed down to her waist like ripples on a lake, and blew back from her face aglow with possibility. The tips of her feet on the upswing just barely brushed the bottoms of clouds, not disturbing in the least the majestic patch of sky, the idyllic landscape.

Once she ceased her pumping, the swing slowed to a rest. A light wind caressed her bare arms and legs, lifting up the gossamer threads of the rich amber and mauve antique frock that adorned her body. Off in the distance a handsome courtier approached steadily on his pure white steed, intent on capturing the incandescent maiden and claiming her for his own.

THE END

ALSO BY JANET GARBER

Non Fiction Book

I Need a Job, Now What? (Silver Lining Books, 2001) re-released as Getting a Job, Silver Lining Books, Barnes & Noble Basics 2003), and available on audiotape

Fiction

The Flap of a Single Wing, Writing Tomorrow, 2013

Paris 1976, Up, Do Anthology, Spider Road Press, 2014,

Secrets, Bohemia Journal, 2014 AND Some Kind of Hurricane, 2016

Mamie Mine, Apologues of Erotica, 2014

Memory Box, Contrapositions, 2014 AND InfectiveINk, 2015

Company Wife, When Women Waken, 2014

Shishkosh, Newtown Literary, 2014

Losing Face, Pen2Paper website, 2014

Werewolves, Beware! Sinner Saints' Growing Pains anthology, Horrified Press, 2015

Are You My Son? Zimbell Press, Dark Monsters anthology, 2016.

Undercover Cat, Forge Literary Journal, May 2016

Poetry

"Two Aspirins and a Cat in the Morning," Viral Cat Press, 2010, AND Pets Across America 2011 AND On Velvet Feet Anthology, 2013 AND In the Questions, Spider Road Press anthology. Nominated for a Pushcart Prize.

"Too Late in the Day to be a Cat?" Hazard Cat (2010).

"Just Get Off the Bus, Already!" Caesura, 2014 (Canada)

"In My Heyday," Minerva Rising, 2014

"The World is Cruel," Heyday Magazine, 2014

"Hunger," Minerva Rising blog, 2015

"Trees in a Hurricane," Rainbow Journal, 2015

"A Boy Leaves His Mother," www.cyclamensandswords.com, under Poetry 2, August 2015

Essays and Reviews
"The Joys of Tantehood," New York Times, 2001

"Too Late: My Son the Procrastinator," Working Mother Magazine, 2012 AND Monkey Star anthology on Babysitters and Tantrums, 2016

"On Perseverance," Minerva Rising, January 2014

"Success Story," Writers Weekly, June 2014

"Nothing Lasts Forever," Mamalode, January 2016

75+ book reviews for, NeworldReview.com (2009-Present); Simply Charly, InReads

Film reviews for Senior Film Files, Stage&Cinema

Journalism
100+ articles for Wall Street Journal Vertical File, Journal of Career Planning and Employment, Careers and the DisAbled, Diversity Magazine, Jewish Week, New York Post career column, Woman's Own, Women's News, Long Island Boating World, Journal News (1990-2000).

READERS' GUIDE

1. What role does an Approach-Avoidance conflict play in the Melie/Ted romance? Melie says, "But humans can't stop themselves from playing games, can they?" Do you agree?

2. What sartorial mistake does Melie make vis-à-vis Merry Terry? And at the Victoriana Ball?

3. Why do employees at Axis Mundi rejoice when Merry Terry expires? What specific actions do they hold against her?

4. What is revealed to be the motive for the murder? Did you think that Melie might have done it?

5. What sort of future do you predict for Melie? Will she stay with Ted? Why/Why not?

6. Why should Melie and Ted and Sheila take a trip to Alaska?

7. Name the three gouramis of the Employment Office. What does Melie hope to learn from them? Is she successful?

8. Can you identify the Pre-Raphaelite painting hanging in Melie's apartment as described by Melie and Ted?

9. What's the chief cause of Melie's meltdown? Other contributing causes? What would be a trigger for you?

10. If you were in Melie's ballet slippers, how would you handle the stress?

11. Why is Ted so noncommittal? A bit unfaithful? So tongue tied?

12. Melie lets her work slide. How come? She prides herself on being Ms. Fix-it. Why doesn't she seek out Keisha Anne Woods after Sukie sends her packing? Or investigate Cherry Lum's claim of racial discrimination? Or seek to dethrone Babs' Dr. Needles?

13. What mistakes does Melie make in her relationships with men? With people in general? She blames her parents—is that reasonable?

14. Who is your favorite character and why? Your least favorite? What do you think about Gladys? Would she be an impediment to you in establishing a new relationship?

15. Have you ever had a boss like Merry Terry or Doug Milty? How did you handle them? Did you ever have a boss who was worse?

ACKNOWLEDGEMENTS

To—

My husband, Shelly, for his unwavering support, love and patience.

My talented buddies in both Gabe Tatela's Westchester Writers' Group and Linda Spear's Somers Library Group

My fellow writers on Zoetrope and Gotham Writers Workshop and FanStory

My first readers: Angele Rugen, Sherry Friedman, Irina Plyas, Marguerite Busetti

My former WSJ editor, Tony Lee, now VP Editorial at SHRM, who continues to support me whether I'm writing journalism or fiction.

My editor, Carol Gaskin/Editorial Alchemy, who taught me so much about writing fiction while commenting on an early draft of *Dream Job*.

MY SINCEREST THANKS!

To my thirty-year career in HR—

When I went to college, women had to wear dresses to class and the only major preparing one for business was accounting. An English/French major who wanted to write, I went to work in the real world of publishing but was soon disillusioned. My fantasy of course was that I'd be given the opportunity to write and from there I'd become an author. My boss told me if I put in five years proofreading punctuation, I might be given the chance to write a paragraph of copy. I quit and became a caseworker before going to graduate school.

Here and there I interviewed for "Personnel" positions. Evidently I did not have the "look." Instead I worked as a French-English secretary and one of my jobs morphed into a quasi HR role. I cycled through wine and spirits, manufacturing, mortgage banking, healthcare, and continuing legal education.

HR suited me to a tee. In my various roles, culminating as Chief HR Office, I managed to combine everything that mattered to me. Writing, teaching, counseling. I could be as creative as my bosses permitted and was rewarded for enriching the daily lives of our employees. Occasionally I thought, as Melie does, *What? They pay me for this?*

Yes, HR is stressful, particularly if staffing is not adequate or personalities and visions clash. For me it was a wonderful career that allowed me to write two books. The first contained all the accumulated "wisdom" I'd been itching to impart to jobseekers I'd interviewed over the years. *Dream Job* displays all the behind-the-scenes mayhem that sometimes threatens to break out. HR practitioners often are forced to be humorless, to act as the police in their company, setting down policies and procedures and making sure wrongdoers get appropriate punishment. That's not the fun part. The fun part is belonging to an entity devoted to accomplishing some good in the world and being in a position to help your staff achieve their best in a positive, nurturing and creative environment.

34899305R00107

Made in the USA
Middletown, DE
09 September 2016